A STOLEN KISS

He intrigued her. He was a blatant contradiction of everything she was so sure of in people. One moment he was an arrogant rake, the next a gentle caring man. Just who was this wild London beau?

She could hear her cousins chatting in the background, but it was a buzz of noise she wanted to filter out. For the moment she wanted only to talk to this man with the twinkling blue eyes.

"Whatever I may think of you today or tomorrow, I *know* you were a hero yesterday," answered Maxie.

He laughed and inclined his head. "Ah, now that sounds as if you read gothic novels, Miss Tarnover."

"That is because I do read and enjoy them as well," she smiled amiably. "However, the truth is you saved my Junior, and I am very grateful."

He had not yet released her fingers, and now brought up her hand so that her wrist was exposed. He bent and gently placed a kiss on her wrist. She trembled and he immediately released her hand. Their eyes met and she was aware, all too aware of the electricity that suddenly shot through her entire body. Quietly, almost seductively he said, "I am very glad I was on hand to assist you."

ZEBRA'S REGENCY ROMANCES
DAZZLE AND DELIGHT

A BEGUILING INTRIGUE   (4441, $3.99)
by Olivia Sumner

Pretty as a picture Justine Riggs cared nothing for propriety. She dressed as a boy, sat on her horse like a jockey, and pondered the stars like a scientist. But when she tried to best the handsome Quenton Fletcher, Marquess of Devon, by proving that she was the better equestrian, he would try to prove Justine's antics were pure folly. The game he had in mind was seduction — never imagining that he might lose his heart in the process!

AN INCONVENIENT ENGAGEMENT   (4442, $3.99)
by Joy Reed

Rebecca Wentworth was furious when she saw her betrothed waltzing with another. So she decides to make him jealous by flirting with the handsomest man at the ball, John Collinwood, Earl of Stanford. The "wicked" nobleman knew exactly what the enticing miss was up to — and he was only too happy to play along. But as Rebecca gazed into his magnificent eyes, her errant fiancé was soon utterly forgotten!

SCANDAL'S LADY   (4472, $3.99)
by Mary Kingsley

Cassandra was shocked to learn that the new Earl of Lynton was her childhood friend, Nicholas St. John. After years at sea and mixed feelings Nicholas had come home to take the family title. And although Cassandra knew her place as a governess, she could not help the thrill that went through her each time he was near. Nicholas was pleased to find that his old friend Cassandra was his new next door neighbor, but after being near her, he wondered if mere friendship would be enough . . .

HIS LORDSHIP'S REWARD   (4473, $3.99)
by Carola Dunn

As the daughter of a seasoned soldier, Fanny Ingram was accustomed to the vagaries of military life and cared not a whit about matters of rank and social standing. So she certainly never foresaw her *tendre* for handsome Viscount Roworth of Kent with whom she was forced to share lodgings, while he carried out his clandestine activities on behalf of the British Army. And though good sense told Roworth to keep his distance, he couldn't stop from taking Fanny in his arms for a kiss that made all hearts equal!

Available wherever paperbacks are sold, or order direct from the Publisher. Send cover price plus 50¢ per copy for mailing and handling to Penguin USA, P.O. Box 999, c/o Dept. 17109, Bergenfield, NJ 07621. Residents of New York and Tennessee must include sales tax. DO NOT SEND CASH.

Masquerade Waltz
Claudette Williams

ZEBRA BOOKS
KENSINGTON PUBLISHING CORP.

dedicated to my love, RTC

ZEBRA BOOKS are published by

Kensington Publishing Corp.
850 Third Avenue
New York, NY 10022

Zebra and the Z logo Reg. U.S. Pat. & TM Off.

First Printing: January, 1995

Printed in the United States of America

Chapter One

Lady Waremont patted her silver curls into place and sighed wearily. She touched a spot on the sofa beside her and coaxed in dulcet tones, "Come darling, a moment of your time."

Lord Waremont was a loving son. He had taken on the watchful care of his mother five years ago when his father had died. There were those who had set out lures to win his heart and finally decided he would give his love to no female but his mother. However, even she could not control his independent, gypsy-wandering nature.

Today he mistrusted her purpose in commanding his presence and eyed her warily as he took the proffered seat, "There, madam, I am sitting. But be careful, my dear, I can just as easily be on my feet and rushing for the door ..." There was teasing in his tone, but the warning hung about the words all the same reminding her that he was well used to ordering his own life.

His mother answered him easily, "Now, why in heavens name would you want to do such a silly thing? I merely want to spend a little time with you before you go gadding about with Kinnaid to inspect the property he has just inherited."

"If it is time you want, dearest, I am pleased to oblige. However, if you mean to harp about marriage again . . ."

"Harp, indeed!" sniffed his mother, touching her silver curls once more. "I am getting on in years, and you"—she raised her hand accusingly for emphasis—"are nearing your thirtieth birthday—next month! But, it certainly is not marriage and grandchildren that I wish to speak to you about, Seth."

"No? Is it not, love? What then *do* you want to speak to me about?" The suspicion crossed his mind that his mother was about to involve him in something he would not like. However, his blue eyes twinkled as he watched her play her part.

"Dearest, you remember I mentioned to you that my carriage broke down last month on my way home from Hastings?"

"Yes," he answered giving her no leeway.

She must have expected him to be difficult, but she proceeded glibly, "Yes, well . . . you may also recall that I was in a bit of a bind as we were told the carriage would take some days to be repaired."

"Yes."

"As it happened, the nearest village was Rye, and while my coachman was there attempting to make arrangements with the hostelry, a local family—Huntly was the name—overheard my sorry state of affairs. He was kind enough to fetch me to his home, where I was very nicely received and kept by his family for more than a week. A delightful family, all very kind you see—"

"I recall your mentioning this to me, Mother," he said, smiling at her. "So why don't you tell me what you want, and have done?"

"Yes, well . . . there you are," returned his mother. "You know the whole and now that you will be in Rye with Kinnaid, you may stop by and pay your respects on my behalf. It is the least you could do. Also, you may take a gift to Mrs. Huntly for me; a lovely Sevres dish."

He eyed his mother thoughtfully. She was a cunning piece. Just what was all this about? Well, he would do the polite for her when he was in Rye. What choice had he? "Right then, Mother. You may rest easy. I shall deliver your gift and your gratitude to these people when I arrive in Rye."

"Thank you, my love." Lady Waremont smiled sweetly.

The inhabitants of Huntly Grange had no idea that a discussion of this nature had taken place between Lady Waremont and her only son. However, Mrs. Huntly was all too aware of the fact that Lady Waremont was an influential noblewoman, the very pink of the *haute ton*. Mrs. Huntly also knew that the lady was the mother of one of London's great marriage prizes, Seth, Lord Waremont, also known as rake Waremont.

Mr. Huntly and his wife had a daughter whose dowry

was certainly adequate, but not stunning. Also, while Miss Huntly was quite a pretty young woman, she was no devastating beauty. However, here was Mrs. Huntly's chance. If she could just get her husband to allow her to take her daughter, Claire, to London, all doors would be opened by Lady Waremont.

Of this fact, Mrs. Huntly was absolutely certain. The lady had been so very grateful to them for entertaining her while her coach was being repaired. She had spent one week with them and seemed a very dear, sweet woman. Thus, Mrs. Huntly went to the study to seek out her husband, her heart was filled with determination.

Mr. Huntly heard his wife's scheme described at length. He heard her out with patience and understanding. However, he deplored this sort of female cunning, and he told her so in strong terms. She proceeded to plead. He held up his large hand and held his ground. She shifted to scolding, and he stood in quiet withdrawal.

Mr. Huntly was a simple man with simple tastes and needs. His wife had never really been truly in love with him. In fact, he was aware she had always felt she had married beneath her station. He knew that she wanted more than their easy country social life for their dear daughter. He was a gentle character who had learned to do without passion in the hopes of peace in his home. He adored his two lovely children Claire and Freddy. And, he knew beyond doubt that his wife's ambitions were not shared by his daughter. What to do? How could he stop his wife from doing this to all of them? To oppose her would mean an end to his well-ordered and peaceful existence. It was always so whenever he chose to stand his ground. He sighed, realizing he must stand firm for Claire's happiness.

Thus, he stated in a manner all his own, "Claire is not going to London for a Season. Now, I must go." So saying he scooped up his gloves and hat from his desk and stomped hurriedly out of his study.

His wife watched him go in silence and her eyes narrowed. He could be stubborn at times. Perhaps, just perhaps, she could convince Claire to work on him?

She rushed after him and caught him up in the hall, "Darling ... at least tell me you will think about it."

"No," he answered straight forwardly.

"How can you be so obstinate when your daughter's happiness is at stake?"

"Claire will manage. She has no wish to have a London Season," he snapped.

"Nonsense. Every young woman wishes a London Season. It is natural." She lowered her lashes in a manner she was sure he had always liked.

He watched her play her trick. She was still quite a handsome woman, though she had grown rather plump, more than was pleasing. Yet even now, after all these years, his heart could be wrenched by her smile. He sighed again. "Claire does not wish to go to London. She has often said so."

"Yes, but, dear—"

"Not now, my love." He turned sharply on his heel and left his wife frustrated at his back.

This time she allowed him to escape. There were

times when there was absolutely no reaching him. Oddly enough, she was not angry with him. He was a good man and though she had never experienced a grand passion, she did like him very much. Moreover, privately she was a bit nervous about her newest scheme. Here in Rye, she was considered a grande dame. In London, she would be insignificant and she knew this, yet, she felt that she owed it to her daughter to make a push to have her meet Lord Waremont now that they had an entré through his mother. What to do? Think, she told herself, I must just think this one out!

Maxie rushed across the moors taking a short-cut home. Her day-gown of brown muslin hugged her form and though it was school-girlish and out of date, it could not shield her loveliness. Her long black hair fell about her shoulders and hung in loose disorderly curls to her trim waist. Short black wisps fringed her forehead and ears. Her eyes were the color of violets, large and full with mischief.

Stopping, she called to the collie and the young man running full speed ahead of her, "Freddy, you wretch! Your legs are so much longer than mine. Give me time to breathe. Poor old Melody, just look at her. She is panting and certainly she's tired." Maxie patted the elderly collie who had plopped down on the tall grass and now rolled over to moan and groan as she gave her back a scratch.

"Good girl," Maxie said laughingly.

Freddy was sixteen. It is an age one should never take

lightly. He had suddenly sprouted in height, opinions and needs that made him ever restless. Maxine Tarnover was only his cousin, but, she was more sister to him than his own sister, Claire. Both Maxine and Claire were eighteen, but, only Maxie had always been at his side. She was real, she was someone he could always go to when the world tilted off balance. He slowed to a stop and laughed at her, "Yes, but, if we aren't home soon we shall be in for a dreadful lecture, and well you know it!"

"What I know beyond argument is that if I don't catch my breath, here and now, my lad, I shall collapse. Do you want that on your head, Frederick of Huntly?"

"You were wont to pass me only a short time ago . . ." mused Freddy.

"That was before you sprouted wings, my buck!" Maxie reached out and took his long arm. "There now, walk for a while. We shall do."

They both looked up at the sky and then at each other to laugh for it surely looked like heavy rain was about to descend. In unison they said to one another, *"We hope!"*

Maxie released her cousin's arm and smiled at him as she walked briskly at his side. There was something they had to discuss, but, she was unsure as how to bring it up. It would be a sore subject and she wasn't even sure she was completely in the right of it. With some reserve she asked, "Freddy . . . you've been spending a great deal of time down at the quay in Rye, haven't you?"

"Hmmm, it has made the summer passable," he answered casually.

"You like Captain Toby very much, don't you?"

"Don't you?" Freddy returned in some surprise. They had both spent some magnificent days with Toby the summer before.

"Freddy, don't avoid the question with one of your own. I asked you first."

He laughed, "I like Toby."

"Yes, I do too. He is certainly a charming old rogue, but, you should not be spending all of your time with him."

"I don't. Spend most of my time with *you.*" Freddy laughed as he put up his hand. "Deplorable habit, but, there you are."

Maxie smiled. "You exaggerate greatly. Let us speak frankly with each other. We always have in the past."

"Aye, but I am nearly a man, and there are some things a gentleman does not discuss with a lady. Now, as much as my mother would like you to still play and dress the part of a schoolgirl, *you* are very much a lady."

"I shall not play games with you Freddy. If you don't wish to discuss Toby with me, don't, but do not treat me as less than a friend." Maxie's chin was up.

Freddy eyed her for a long moment. "Oh, very well, what then?"

"Nought, but this. I happen to know that fishing is not Toby's main source of income." She added quietly, "What say you, my buck?"

Once more Freddy eyed her. "Rather thought you guessed that. However, what Toby does to earn his bread is none of our affair."

"Is it not?" asked Maxie, her dark violet eyes questioning him gravely.

"No, it has nothing to do with me."

"And will it remain in that realm, Freddy. Nothing to do with you?"

"Blister it, girl! Don't you know that I can draw the line?"

"Can you Freddy? Good, then, we are agreed that you can. But do you want to?"

Melody had discovered a twig and brought it to drop at their feet. Without answering, Freddy picked it up and threw it for the collie to fetch. Then turning to his cousin, he said, "Come on then. We have tarried here too long."

So saying he broke into a jog, and with a shake of her pretty head, Maxine followed.

Chapter Two

Waremont regarded Kinnaid thoughtfully as he relaxed against the squabs of his friend's luxurious traveling coach. Their riding horses had been tethered at the boot and ambled along easily in their wake. Their progress was slower then his lordship was used to, but the weather was inclement and the sky dusky, making swifter travel unadvisable.

Outside the changing scenery had moved from hills of rolling woods and lush green farmland into sloping downs of wildflowers and deep purple heather. Despite the gloom, it was glorious and Waremont recalled the days of his youth when his father had taken him to Romney Marsh and filled his head with tales of ghosts and smugglers. It looked as though nothing had changed. A vast flatland of marsh met their eyes and excited the imagination. Waremont could smell the saltwater and it made him anxious to quit the coach.

Sir Leigh Kinnaid felt his friend's scrutiny and returned the look warily. "What then? What is it?"

"I was just thinking what a lucky thing it was that cousin of yours decided to pop off at last and leave you with Romney property. Damned good sport here."

"By Jupiter, Seth. That is a damned unfeeling thing to say!" reproved Kinnaid.

"Why? He was old and you hardly knew the fellow. Besides, he had no choice, the estate was entailed to the next in line and that was you. *Sir* Leigh. Doesn't sound quite right. Your name should have been John, or Richard." Waremont laughed easily.

"Well, it just ain't the thing, talking like that," returned Kinnaid. "And I like the sound of Sir Leigh."

Waremont laughed. "By Jove. So do I."

"Damned glad to get out of London. That little Italian beauty was just about to corner me. I felt it, and her count of a father was pushing for it all the while."

"Well, what you wanted with such as that, is more than I can fathom, Leigh. What did you think to do with her? You can't bed a gently born maid without offering her your hand in marriage."

"Didn't bed her. Flirted . . . just for the fun of it. She was quite a delectable piece you know, very hard to resist."

"Well, if I hadn't saved you that last night when you were out in the garden with her you would now be an engaged man."

"Don't I know it," snorted Kinnaid. "But, I'm not the only one that was taken in by a girl's charms. What of you with that fair child up in Scotland?"

"I wasn't even dazzled, only attracted. Knew what I was doing all the while. Besides, *she* wasn't a virgin."

"Aha! So you did have her."

"No, I did not, but that was because I liked her. Didn't want to hurt the poor girl when I knew she was in earnest."

"I hear the girls in Rye are beauties . . . every one!"

Waremont laughed. "Well, we shall soon find out!"

Maxie called out sharply, "Freddy wait! I can't run anymore, I'm out of breath."

"Zounds, girl. We'll never make it in time for dinner if we don't run."

"Yes, we will. We can take the shortcut through Abbey Woods."

"Isn't that full of briars?"

"No, it isn't. I know a path . . . come on." Max looked for her collie and called out, "Melody, here girl!"

A moment later they were scurrying through the woods. It was growing dark and rain threatened. As they reached the opening onto the road they were met by a low mist. Max could hear the snort of a horse and pulled up short putting a hand to Freddy to stop him, but Melody rushed forward onto the road, straight into the path of two riders, and whelped as she was caught by flying hooves.

"What have you done?" Maxine cried as she ran forward and hovered over her collie.

Melody got to her feet at that moment and shook herself. She appeared stunned but, she didn't look as if she was seriously hurt. Freddy dropped down beside the dog and rubbed her long nose. "Eh, then girl."

One of the riders was off his horse and moving towards the collie, who very amiably limped to the new-comer and sniffed a greeting. Waremont patted the collie vigorously and announced, "There she'll do."

Maxine took exception to his casual attitude. "No thanks to you. What can you have been thinking, charging about in the mist?"

"If you had not allowed your dog to run onto the road, my dear, you would not now have an injured pet."

"I am not your dear, and I did not know anyone would be barreling through the mist on what we consider a backroad!"

"Which only goes to display your inexperience and your limited knowledge."

"Please," cut in the second man, "we are very sorry if your collie has been injured. As you say we should not—"

"Now this is too much," snapped the other man, seeming much incensed. "Don't go on, my friend. We were not charging about and this girl is out of her ken."

Kinnaid considered his friend for a moment. There was some truth to this, but he had no desire to continue this argument. He simply wished to continue on their way. Their coach was slowly approaching and he tried another idea.

"Look, our coach is here. May we offer you, and your dog of course, a ride home?"

Freddy moved to gratefully accept, however, Maxine stalled him, with an abrupt, "No, thank you." So saying she called for Melody and, with a look at her cousin, marched off, the words "Damned snip of a girl. They grow them rude in Romney" ringing in her ears.

Freddy grinned, shrugged and followed in her wake.

Some ten minutes later Maxine and Freddy entered their home via the kitchen door. There they found the cook waving a ladle at them and saying ominously that her darlings were in for it now, as the mistress was in a tither over their tardiness. They kissed the large woman and thanked her for her concern.

Freddy added glibly, "Never you mind, Cookie love, Mama has to learn that Max and I are adults and cannot forever be kept to her apron strings."

His sister entered the kitchen at that moment clasping her hands and exclaimed, "Thank goodness, you are here. Papa is in the dining room calming mother, but she is in a rare mood and I fear it is all my fault."

"Nonsense," said Maxine taking Claire's hand. "How can that be?"

"Never mind now. We must go right away, so that dinner can be served without any further delay." She looked at Maxine's soiled gown and sighed, "I must say it is no other's fault but Mama's for the way you behave. If she must treat you like a schoolgirl and dress you like a schoolgirl, she should not be surprised when you behave like a schoolgirl. You are only a few months younger than I, and should be brought out as I was. I have often heard Papa say so."

"Ah, but she is Papa's blood relation, not Mama's," said Freddy meaningfully.

Mr. Huntly was in the midst of asking his wife to be patient when the three young people entered the modestly furnished dining room. His son going forward to take his mother's hands and place a kiss upon her cheek. Wise lad, Mr. Huntly thought and then could not help but note the contrast between his daughter and his niece. Though his wife dressed Maxie beneath her years, though she was a rough and tumble minx with her black tresses in disarray, she was certainly a beauty! No one could deny his Claire was quite pretty. However, Claire's quiet style, even her fair coloring and feminine elegance could not compare to Maxine's wild loveliness. He had no doubt that this was why his wife refused to bring her out. She wanted no competition for their own lovely daughter.

He often sighed over the problem. Maxine was his only sister's child. It was his duty to care for her and see that she was given every opportunity to find a husband and have a life for herself. He had taken what little funds her poor parents had left to her at the time of their deaths, and he had invested it with some excellent results. He meant this to be her dowry.

He stood back now and watched as both Claire and Maxine begged his wife to forgive them their tardiness. He sighed when he saw his wife take on a steely look and was pleasantly surprised when she suddenly waved her hand at them and declared, "Children, children, afterall I am no demon. Sit, before our dinner is too cold to enjoy."

Chapter Three

Morning arrived in Romney Marsh dispelling the rains of the evening. A bright September sun welcomed Waremont as he moved to his bedroom window and looked out on the vast gardens of Kinnaid's newly acquired estate.

There was a scratch at the door and without turning around he called a welcome, knowing by instinct that it would be Kinnaid. He was not wrong.

"Up are you? Good. Come on, I mean to inspect m'new land. The ride will do you some good."

"Ay, I suppose." Waremont moved towards his friend with a smile. "No doubt we should call on Mr. Huntly and pay our respects so that I may face my mother in good form?"

Kinnaid eyed Waremont gravely. "Of course we must visit Huntly Grange. I have already taken their direction from Wiggens." Then in a conspiratorial voice he added, "Wiggens is an odd sort of chap for a butler.

He's been here forever I take it. Knows more than he lets on, I'd wager."

"Now what in thunder does that mean?"

"Been to the cellar, speaks for itself," said Kinnaid secretively. "Show you later."

"Blister it, my man, you will show me now," grinned Waremont.

Maxie entered her uncle's study at his request and stood nervously, her hands clasped behind her back as she eyed him speculatively. She knew her uncle was fond of her, but he rarely displayed affection or attention. Summoning her to his study was highly unusual and she could not help but feel uneasy about the business. Had she done something particularly irregular?

Mr. Huntly looked up from his papers and noted that Maxine's pretty black hair was tied with a worn blue ribbon at the nape of her neck. She wore a simple blue muslin day gown with an old white bibbed collar. He frowned and pointed to her gown. "Do you not have anything better to wear my dear?"

Maxine's hands went over her midriff and she blushed. "I beg your pardon, Uncle." To say anything else would be to openly blame her aunt which she could not do.

Mr. Huntly was quick to understand this and sighed. "Never mind, child. I am at fault for not having noticed earlier. Your wardrobe is sadly lacking. I have no intention of allowing this situation to continue. Your mother was such a lovely woman and so well dressed; it would grieve her to see you in virtual rags. You will go into town today. Take my curricle and order some gowns more in keeping with your age and the fashion."

Maxine was momentarily overcome and stood still a long moment.

Her uncle went to her and put a folded paper in her hands. "You give this to that shop Claire frequents in town. Have them make up a complete wardrobe for you. Buy what you need, everything from ribbons to slippers. And a riding habit as well. It is time you stopped riding about the countryside in britches."

Maxine was overwhelmed. She couldn't find her voice and instead simply hugged him. Then she said, "Uncle . . . thank you."

"Nonsense. Don't think I don't know m'duty, child. Besides, I have a notion to see both m'girls sporting the fancy." He patted her on the back. "There now . . . go on."

Maxine kissed his cheek and hurried off, stopping only at the door to whisper another heartfelt thank you.

Mr. Huntly waved her off and smiled thoughtfully. Well now old boy, he told himself in the quiet of the study, you will have hell to pay when the missus finds out. Never mind. What could he do? Conscience will out. So be it.

Riding abreast of one another, Waremont and Kinnaid halted their horses atop a hill of tall grass. "From the old survey my man gave me, that wall separates me from Huntly Grange," Kinnaid pointed out.

"Nice little parcel," commented Waremont. "Damned beautiful country this."

"So different from our properties in the Cotswolds. Look there." Kinnaid pointed off in the near distance. There was a sandy country road at the bottom of the long sloping hill. The road was shaded by the wide tall oaks that lined the avenue, however a neat little curricle pulled by a large bay horse could be seen. "Isn't that the girl whose collie you stepped on yesterday?"

Waremont had already seen that it was. She looked different now, sitting up straight, in full command of her vehicle, and there was something else he noticed that he had not noticed yesterday; she certainly had the form of a woman, a very provocative woman! "I didn't step on her collie. The poor thing got under my horse's hooves and well you know it!"

"It's the same thing. No matter. Wonder who she is? Looks like she is headed for the Grange." Then as a thought struck him, "Seth! Damnation old boy. She must be the Miss Huntly! You've stepped on the Huntly's dog!"

"Confound it! Stop saying *I* stepped on the dog. I didn't! Besides, it was a blistering accident. Deuced nuisance!" He shook his head woefully. "Now I've got to go and do the polite with this hanging over me."

"Wouldn't want to be in your shoes old boy, that's for certain."

"You have been often enough," grinned Waremont, recalling a lark they had enjoyed only months ago.

Kinnaid reminisced for a moment and sighed. "Ah,

the lovely Caroline of Scotland. That was quite different, and well you know it."

"How so? You passed yourself off as Lord Waremont, titled and wealthy and won the lady of your heart." Waremont laughed.

"She wasn't quite the lady of my heart. She was the woman of the moment." He eyed Waremont accusingly. "And as I recall, it was you who prompted me to present myself off as you. Said the lady hankered after a title. Said all was fair in love and war and some other balderdash."

"Well, it worked. The lovely went straight to your bed, did she not?"

"Deuced dangerous that was." Kinnaid shook his head. "When she returned the next day with that fishwife she had for a mother who demanded that I marry the girl, I thought I was finished."

"You were safe. She and her mother were after a title. I knew they would have no use for you once they discovered you were not Lord Waremont, titled and rich."

"Yes, well, learned m'lesson even so. Not masquerading as you to win the ladies." Kinnaid shook his fair head and pulled a face. "A bit weary of the game, you know."

Waremont eyed him thoughtfully for a moment. "Pity."

"Seth, what have you buzzing about in that devilish mind of yours?"

"Let us play the game just one more time, Leigh." Waremont suggested slowly. "Think how much fun we could have? Think how we shall laugh over it later?"

"No." Kinnaid said firmly even as he felt himself catching interest in Waremont's scheme.

"You don't mean to live here at your Romney Grange, do you?" Kinnaid hesitated, only because he was leery of Waremont's ability to talk him into something he really shouldn't do. "No. More interested in running my estates in the Cotswolds and living in town. Might visit here now and then. Never know," he added.

"Right. And by the time you visit, no one will remember what you look like," said Waremont.

"Gammon. Everyone would know. Know what?" Kinnaid asked feeling himself in deep waters.

"No one will know if you were me and I were you for just one day? Where is the harm?"

"Aha! Where is the good? Don't see the sport in this one," said Kinnaid adamantly.

"Must save me, Leigh. Do it as a favor to me and I shall owe you one. I have to go to Huntly to pay m'mother's respects, hand over her gift to them and say I didn't mean for my horse to trample their dog. Awkward. Damned awkward." Waremont sighed. "Better if I were you, Sir Leigh, the new owner of Romney. They won't like me. They will say I am too puffed up in my own consequence and never wish to see me—that is you—ever again. We shall return to London and it will be over!"

"You want me to present myself as you? Are you mad?" retorted Kinnaid.

"It will be famous good sport." Waremont grinned. "It is not as though we have never played this game."

"Seth, this is different. We are going to pay your

mother's respects to these people in their own home. Duplicity is no way to repay them."

"Look here, my mother's name impressed them. They have a daughter my mother wishes me to meet. That is the only reason she has asked me to pay them this visit. I am heartily sick of being chased as a marriage prize."

"Then it isn't because of the dog?" Kinnaid was momentarily diverted.

"Absurd fellow. Would I really give a fig about that? Just meant to get your attention. Come on Leigh, let them throw their daughter at your feet. You will like that, won't you?"

"No, by thunder! I would not like that at all. That little girl we met yesterday, she was a spitfire, a termagant that I should like to stay well away from."

"Right then, Leigh, you won't be seeing these people after today. Where is the harm?"

"What if we chance to meet them somewhere?"

"It won't be for years. They'll never remember."

"Don't see that. People remember us. At least they always remember you."

"Leigh, we'll do, don't we always?"

Kinnaid could not deny this. They were considered the very pink of the ton, Waremont was a top sawyer, a Corinthian, and a great gun. There wasn't a man whom Kinnaid knew who wouldn't want to call Waremont friend. However, this was different. He knew that Waremont was itching for excitement. He could see it, but, this, this was something he could feel in his bones might be their total undoing. "Yes, Seth, but I don't like this."

"I have a notion that before we are done you will." A grin took over Waremont's handsome features making him look like a boy out for sport.

Kinnaid smiled and felt some of Waremont's irrepressible humor infect him. "Right then, I suppose we'll have at them, may the Gods forgive us."

"And protect us, my friend, and protect us."

Chapter Four

The Huntly's butler, Peltons, met Maxie at the front door. She stood like an expectant child, her arms full with her packages and he took the liberty of smiling. Peltons had learned to be very fond of Miss Maxine in the six years she had lived at Huntly Grange.

"Well, miss, you have been busy. Here, allow me."

"Thank you, Peltons, I have these in hand, but if you will have the remaining boxes in the curricle taken to my room, then John can take the curricle back to the stable and see to the bay. Thank you ever so much, Peltons."

"Yes, miss." Only the hint of glitter in the elderly man's faded hazel eyes betrayed the great pleasure he felt. He called for a footman to gather the remaining packages and thought it was time the master took notice of his own flesh and blood niece. This sentiment dominated most of the Huntly household. Everyone had been discussing it in the kitchen just that morning. Mrs. Huntly was not pleased but only Martha, Mrs. Huntly's maid, had taken her part in the morning's debate. She said the money would have been better spent on Miss Claire's having a London Season. Humph! Everyone knew that Claire wanted to stay on in Rye. Aye, everyone knew that except her own mother.

Maxie couldn't get to her room fast enough. Once there, she ripped open the first of the packages she had brought with her to hold up a length of forest green material. It was perfect. It would make up into the finest, prettiest, most wonderful morning gown. Better than anything she had ever had. A knock sounded at her door and she called out a welcome. Claire peeped round the door and then exclaimed sweetly, "Maxie . . . you left so early this morning . . . oh Maxie, that is beautiful! She moved to put an arm around her cousin, "That shade of green will look perfect on you with your dark coloring."

Maxie beamed. "Oh Claire, I wanted your help deciding how to have it made up. And wait till you see what else is here and what Madame is making for me for riding—"

"And the ball, Maxie? What color are you having made for the ball?"

The smile vanished from Maxine's face, "I . . . I am not going to the ball."

"What? Why not?"

"Claire, I was not invited." Maxine looked away, "It doesn't matter."

"What do you mean you are not invited? I saw the

invitation myself." Claire shook her head. "You are a silly goose. Why Laura has been your friend for an age. Why would she not invite you?"

"But . . . your mother told me that my name was not on the invitation."

"Mama must have been confused when she told you that. Laura would never have left you off the list."

"No, but perhaps her mother does not—"

"Absurd girl. I saw the invitation myself, I tell you, and your name was written with ours. Mother made an error."

As Maxine seemed doubtful still, Claire took both her hands and said affectionately, "Maxie, Maxie, we will just have to return to Madame's tomorrow and order a ballgown!"

At that moment Mrs. Huntly was on the attack. She had decided to try a new tactic with her unsuspecting husband. She wanted a London Season for her daughter and she meant to get it one way or another. She meant to use the fact that he had just splurged money lavishly on his niece to her advantage. She put on a smile and walked into the study where her husband was enjoying a letter from one of his cronies. He looked up from his reading to find his wife descending upon him and stifled a sigh. He waited for the inevitable and it came in the form of cajolery.

"Hallo, darling, do I interrupt?" Mrs. Huntly asked softly.

Ever gallant Mr. Huntly smiled a warm welcome.

"Not at all, my dear, unless of course you mean to scold me again?"

"Nonsense. What kind of a woman would I be to deny my husband's niece some new clothing? How odd I would look. I am very glad that you noticed that she was all grown up and in need of new dresses. Why, I am utterly humiliated to think that our friends and our surrounding neighbors might have noticed and believed we were neglecting the child."

"Indeed." He was happy to find her so complacent. "Well then, my love. Dare I hope that it is my company you seek?"

She planted herself beside him on their yellow damask sofa and said softly, "Now why would that surprise you?"

"Why indeed?" He chuckled and pinched her full cheek. "There, tell me what it is you need, so that we may be comfortable?"

Peltons appeared at the open door of the library and announced, "Lord Waremont and Sir Leigh Kinnaid."

Mrs. Huntly lost her color and then regained it in force as she looked to her husband in sudden desperation. "Lord Waremont? Here?"

There was no time for more as Kinnaid entered at that moment, closely followed by Waremont. Kinnaid moved towards Mrs. Huntly on the sofa and took her extended hand to bend a perfunctory kiss upon her fingertips. "Mrs. Huntly, what a great pleasure this is to finally meet you."

"My lord, what an unexpected pleasure this is to be sure. I was just this moment thinking about your lovely mother." She turned to her husband, "Mr. Huntly and I so enjoyed having her stay with us though we only had her for one paltry week. Isn't that right darling?"

"Yes, yes, fine woman, fine woman your mother," said Mr. Huntly heartily. He extended his hand and was pleased to find Waremont's grip was solid. He turned to look at Waremont's friend. Fine big strapping man, he thought idly and smiled a welcome, "Well then, you must be the new owner of Romney Grange, Sir Leigh. Heard you were on your way." He chuckled. "Had no notion Waremont here was your friend."

Kinnaid eyed Waremont whose blue eyes glittered with amusement for he could see that Mrs. Huntly was all he imagined she would be. She settled it once and for all when she then hurriedly interjected, "Oh, I must send for Claire." She looked at the man she thought to be his lordship and explained, "Claire is my daughter and got on so well with your mother, that I know she would love to meet you." She moved to pull the bellrope, chattering absurdities all the while.

A moment later Peltons arrived and Mrs. Huntly quietly requested, "Where is my daughter, Peltons, do you know?"

"Yes, madam. She is with Miss Maxine."

"Have her join us here."

"Yes, madam."

"Both of them," added Mr. Huntly jovially. He turned to the gentlemen at hand and explained, "Maxine is my niece."

"Well of course both of them," said Mrs. Huntly attempting to hide her irritation with a half-smile.

Again the gentlemen at hand exchanged glances. Waremont winked at his friend and whispered, "You see. Daughters and nieces will be flung at your feet. Lucky boy."

Maxine had just finished trying on one of her cousin's gowns to see if she wanted it copied in the forest green muslin.

Claire put a finger to her thin lips and said thoughtfully, "Max, come here and sit in front of your mirror. I want to try something with your hair."

Maxine did as she was told and allowed Claire to brush her thick black tresses when a knock sounded at the door and Claire called merrily, "Entré."

Peltons bowed at the threshold of the bedroom and explained that they were wanted in the library. He attempted to impart to them the significance of this by clearing his throat. Max eyed him for a moment and demanded, "Why? What is going on?"

"The master and mistress have visitors. Lord Waremont and Sir Leigh Kinnaid of Romney Grange," he answered portentously.

Maxine started to get up but Claire put a restraining hand on her shoulder and kept her in place. "Your hair, ninny!"

"There is no time," complained Max impatient to be off.

"There is always time. Now, they really can't leave until we arrive, can they? Besides, keep them expectant with anticipation."

Maxine laughed. "Dreadful girl. Games are awful things, but, if you must, then quickly, have at me and let's be done."

Claire entered the room looking etheral in her ivory muslin with her short gold-lit brown hair framing her pretty face in waves. She was tall, slender and certainly graceful. Her sweetness of disposition showed in her clear grey eyes, and her soft smile. Her mother put out a welcoming hand. "Here you are my love." She turned to her guests and said proudly, "My daughter, Claire." Then almost as an afterthought she looked round to politely introduce her niece. She was caught off guard a moment, for Maxine looked more stunning than Mrs. Huntly had thought possible. She had always known what it would be if Maxine were taken out of her schoolgirl trappings, but . . . why now, in one of Claire's best gowns, with Lord Waremont here? She paused to regain her composure before introducing her niece. "Ah . . . and our niece, Maxine Tarnover."

Claire had tied Maxine's black hair at the top of her head. There she had taken the long curls and pinned them about Max's well shaped head in Grecian style. Thick black curls framed Maxine's forehead and tickled her ears. Her borrowed dress, a dark blue muslin had lace trimming at the bodice and at the cuffs of the tight fitting sleeves. Her trim waist was sashed with velvet in the same shade as the gown and the whole displayed her figure to great advantage.

Maxine's violet eyes found Lord Waremont, the real Lord Waremont and she uttered, *"You!"*

All eyes turned to Maxine. However, it was Mrs. Huntly who found her voice first to reprove indignantly. "Maxine! That is certainly no way to greet a guest in our home. Make your apology to Sir Leigh, my child."

Maxine blushed and made a pretty curtsy. "I do beg your pardon, Sir Leigh. I was momentarily caught off guard."

Lord Waremont grinned and turned to Mr. and Mrs. Huntly to explain in patronizing tones. "Please don't blame your niece. Miss Tarnover and I had a very unfortunate meeting yesterday afternoon."

"Indeed," put in Kinnaid hurriedly for he could see that Mrs. Huntly was the sort of person that would scold the girl afterward, "Sir Leigh's horse managed somehow to tangle with Miss Tarnover's collie on the road yesterday afternoon."

"Really?" Mr. Huntly looked concerned. "Frederick never said a word of it to me. Was Melody hurt, Maxine?"

"No, Uncle, she was not . . . at least not seriously, but, she could have been—"

"Nonsense. It is done and Melody is well, so let us put it behind us," stuck in Mrs. Huntly hurriedly. She turned to smile at Kinnaid. "My lord, how long will you be staying in Rye? I do hope you will give us the pleasure of your company at dinner tonight?"

"I merely bear Sir Leigh company while he inspects the Grange and conducts his estate business with his agent." Kinnaid looked towards Waremont for help at this juncture. The charade could not continue throughout an entire dinner? They had to find a way out of this for he could see it was much more complicated than they had supposed.

Waremont was looking at Maxine who felt his eyes on her, but refused to acknowledge his appraisal. It occurred to him that the chit was certainly an interesting mixture of minx and woman. Unable to catch his friend's attention, Kinnaid sighed and turned to find Maxine looking his way. She smiled warmly at him and said in a voice he found sweetly urging, "It was wonderful having Lady Waremont with us. She is a marvelous lady." She eyed him for a moment and then in her candid way remarked, "You are very different from what I imagined."

"I am?" Kinnaid felt warning signals go off in his head.

"Oh yes. Her ladyship often hinted that you were, unconventional, wild, she said, to a fault." Maxine smiled and moved her pretty chin in Waremont's direction. "I don't quite see that. In fact, I think your friend is the wild one. You probably suffer the reputation by association."

"Oh well, I wouldn't judge him by one incident," said Kinnaid feeling very much that he wanted to disappear into the woodwork.

"I wasn't judging," said Maxine softly, wondering in fact if that was what she was doing. "At any rate. It certainly is very nice to meet you, my lord, for I must tell you even in that one short week, I developed a fondness for your lovely mother."

Mrs. Huntly finally disengaged herself and Claire from the man she believed to be Sir Leigh, and positioned herself between her niece and the man she believed to be Lord Waremont. Sir Leigh was all very well, but, he was nought next to the biggest marriage prize in all of London. Casually she managed to say, "Maxine is quite an authority on the history of our village of Rye." She smiled and pushed gently on Maxine's shoulder so that Maxine found herself looking up into the most arresting blue eyes she had ever seen.

"Really?" said Waremont grinning wickedly. He was well able to detect Mrs. Huntly's ploy to win the man she thought to be Waremont for her daughter. He could see that Maxine was reluctant to bear him company in conversation and the devil in him won out. He found himself smiling charmingly at Maxine and saying softly, "Shall we call a truce, you and I?"

"I don't know what you are talking about?" returned the young lady stubbornly. He was a sight too self-assured for her liking.

"Don't you?" He bowed to her and when he unbent, his blue eyes twinkled with humor, "Forgive me. I should not have been racing along the road in the mist. Deuced thoughtless of me."

"Oh, what a self-righteous prig you must think me. Don't we all race along a nice stretch of flat road when we can?" She smiled at him. "I do beg your pardon, Sir Leigh. I did not mean to go on about it forever."

Waremont was momentarily taken off guard. Here was a miss not quite in the ordinary. Schoolgirl one moment, sprig of fashion the next, and suddenly now fair-minded as well? He was intrigued, but, his friend was nudging him for attention. With something of a frown, he turned to Kinnaid. "What is it old fellow?"

"Wants us tonight for dinner." There was a desperate sound in his whispered words, "Do something!"

Waremont grinned boyishly at him, and then turned to Mrs. Huntly to merrily say that they would be happy to accept her invitation.

Mrs. Huntly put her hands together ecstatically, "How very excellent." She moved toward the door. "Please do excuse me. I must send for Cook and revise the menu."

Kinnaid tried to stop her, looking anxiously from Waremont to Mrs. Huntly with something close to panic and did in fact call out, "No, please, do not put your cook to any trouble on our account."

Mrs. Huntly was already at the door and merely laughed as she waved off this objection, saying that menu changes were the veriest nothings, and often done in their busy household. Mr. Huntly eyed his wife's retreating form for he was well acquainted with cook's temperamental personality and knew that his wife would have a supreme work of diplomacy ahead of her.

Claire had been watching Kinnaid for some moments and thought that he looked sadly uneasy about the sudden dinner her mother had presumptuously arranged. She hesitated and then softly said, "My lord, perhaps my mother expects too much of you and Sir Leigh. No doubt you must have other plans for this evening?"

Kinnaid looked into her grey eyes and found himself smiling. "There is nothing we want to do more than dine with you and your lovely family."

There was the flirtation in Sir Leigh's tone and Claire found a sudden interest in her ivory satin slippers before she was able to meet Kinnaid's eyes and say, "You are very gallant, but I know mother is quite forceful ..."

"Not at all." He smiled warmly at her. "Dinner with the Huntlys is something I look forward to very much."

"It was very nice having your mother here with us. She is very lively," returned Claire suddenly feeling uncharacteristically shy.

Sir Leigh Kinnaid frowned for a moment. "Indeed, she would be most distressed to think that after your kindness to her we caused an injury to your dog. I do hope the collie is not seriously hurt."

Claire smiled. "As to that I saw Mel running about earlier this morning looking fit as ever, so you have no concern there." She eyed him curiously. "Only you must know, I hadn't heard a thing from either my brother or Max, so tell me, what happened?"

"Ah, but, a gentleman never tells." Sir Leigh inclined his head and his soft grey eyes twinkled.

"Are you saying the blame lies at my cousin and brother's door?" Claire bantered playfully.

"Accidents are accidents, blame does little good."

"That does not answer my question, my lord."

"Now you will say I am ungallant." He was grinning mischievously.

"No, I would not. However, I shall apply to Max for

my answers and she, my lord, will certainly not withhold them."

"Then I must bow to the lady. Whatever your cousin's version turns out to be, I must accept."

"Well, that is certainly true for I have never known Maxine to lie."

Kinnaid felt himself wince. Lies, soon he would be drowning in them. Why had he allowed Waremont to talk him into this outrageous deception? Why was he coming to dinner to continue the game? It was unforgiveable that they should lie to these good people. At that moment Mrs. Huntly reappeared, noted that her husband and Maxine were engaged in a lively political discussion with the man she believed to be Sir Leigh. Satisfied that they were occupied, she moved in on the man she thought to be Lord Waremont and smiled warmly at him to say, "My dear Lord Waremont, cook was very desirous of knowing your favorite dessert. Luckily, I recalled that your mama enjoyed apple tarts and mentioned that you did as well. I took the liberty of telling her to go ahead and bake them for tonight." She smiled sweetly.

Oh yes, thought Kinnaid, she is looking to trap Waremont for her daughter. He was absolutely right on that score. He found that he did not really like Mrs. Huntly. He looked from her to her husband. He seemed a nice fellow. His daughter, Claire seemed to have a character more in his likeness than her grasping mother's style. Kinnaid looked towards his friend and discovered Waremont engrossed in lively banter with Mr. Huntly and Miss Tarnover. Well, well, there you are, he told himself. He is having a very good time of it, not in the least bit hampered by guilt and it was *his* mother who stayed with these people! So be it. Damn, but Waremont had an exterior of steel. He was the very devil and so he would tell him as soon as they took their leave and were safely on their way!

Chapter Five

Maxine was dressed in britches and one of Freddy's serviceable dark jackets. Her long black hair was tied at the back of her head with string. She was riding her bay gelding across the yellowed grassy fields at a heady pace and her violet eyes were filled with pleasure.

The afternoon had turned dreary and the sky was overcast, but Maxie was filled with a sense of excitement. The morning had been all but perfect. Her new gowns would soon be ready. The visitors they had received had been different from any gentlemen she had ever known. Lord Waremont was a very pleasant man. He was modest, he was fun, and he did not at all seem like the man his mother had so often spoken of during her stay. In fact, there wasn't anything wild or rakish about him. Sir Leigh, on the other hand, was though extremely charming, something of an arrogant blade, and seemed much more about the town than did Lord Waremont. Odd that. She couldn't believe they had actually accepted her aunt's invitation to dinner. She was very certain that Lord Waremont and his friends were used to very different entertainment and would no doubt be thoroughly bored before the evening's end.

Well, that was not for some hours yet to come and now she was off to visit John. The anticipation of this excursion had her nearly out of breath as she reined her gelding down to a walk and surveyed the thatched cottage at the bottom of the sloping field. She patted her horse's wide strong neck and urged him forward, as she reached up to wave to the plump woman standing in the garden and looking her way. Mrs. Baxley smiled warmly and returned Maxine's greeting heartily. "Aye there, child. Leave your horse in the paddock. Then come to the kitchen for some of m'fine blackberry tea. Cookie baked some biscuits fresh this morning."

Maxine's smile wobbled. "Oh, is John . . . I mean is Doctor Wiltshire not at home then?"

The elderly housekeeper smiled and winked. "No love, but, he will be. In the meantime, Cook and I will have to do." She waved Maxine off saying, "You'll have to see to your own horse for Remy is off on an errand for the doctor."

Maxine laughed, "I am very well used to caring for my own animal, but I shall require two of Cookie's very wonderful biscuits when I am done, and with that treat in mind I shall only be a minute!"

Mrs. Baxley smiled fondly and advised Maxine that she was a saucy piece.

It didn't take Max long to undo her girth and slide the saddle off her horse's back. She placed this on the weathered fence, touched her horse's chest and, reassured that he was not overly hot, unbridled him and allowed him water. A moment later she was pulling off her kid gloves and peeping in at the quaint kitchen. "Hmmm, the tea smells so inviting!"

"There child, sit and be comfortable," said Mrs. Baxley patting a wooden chair beside her own.

Cookie's smile curved in her wide plump cheeks as she raised her cup of tea to Maxie. "I won't be sitting wit ye Maxie m'dear. I've got this stew to look after, but, go on it won't keep me from chatting all the same."

Maxie plopped herself down and took up the proffered cup thankfully. Mrs. Baxley regarded her a moment and then ventured a casual inquiry. "Did you hear that the new owner of Romney Grange has arrived?"

"He came to call, but my first meeting with him was not a very good one," said Maxine.

"Ouh now, how is that?" Mrs. Baxley's fine grey brow was up and Cookie stopped her vigorous ministrations at her large black pot to look at Maxine.

"His horse stepped on Melody and I am afraid I was terribly rude to him. To be fair, I must admit that I should not have let poor Mel run onto the road like that, but, then he should not have been galloping through the mist either."

"Oh, lass, lass . . . tis time you left the hoyden behind. Why, just look at you now. You're dressed like a boy and roaming the countryside unattended." Mrs. Baxley shook her head.

Maxine laughed naughtily. "*That* is why I *am* dressed like a boy. Besides, everyone about is used to my ways. No one minds."

Cookie snorted. "You listen to Mrs. Baxley. She be in the right of it and I'll tell ye another thing on top of that, tis time that aunt of yers did somethin' about yer clothing!"

"Oh! That is my other news. I have an entire new wardrobe." Maxine beamed. "Uncle arranged it all!"

"And that was long overdue!" said a familiar masculine voice at Maxine's back.

She hurriedly, excitedly turned round to find a welcome gentleman standing at the threshold of the kitchen doorway. He was of good height. His hair framed his attractive face in shades of auburn and silver. His brows were thick, his eyes hazel, and his nose aquiline. His smile seemed to bring his features together pleasantly. He was Doctor John Wiltshire.

Maxine jumped up merrily. "Doctor John! You are back. There is so much we must talk about."

"That is all very well, and so we shall, if you calm yourself into some semblance of the young lady that I know you are," said the doctor gravely. There was no twinkle in his soft-colored eyes to belie the words.

It was his major fault, thought Maxie sorrowfully. He would be so perfect if only he had a bit more humor in his character. They got on so well together, but she knew he wanted to change her if he could. He was no more than two and thirty, but he acted as if he were in his dotage and she but a child of ten or eleven. It was ridiculous. "If you don't ask the impossible, you won't be disappointed," teased Maxie, her own violet eyes twinkling very much.

Doctor John's nature was staid. It often astounded

him that he found himself so devastatingly attracted to such a madcap of a girl. She was young, he told himself, she could be trained to be a doctor's wife . . . in time. At any rate, he always found it very difficult to resist her ready smile, so warm, so inviting. He seemed to want her more each day and he knew, felt very certain she was not indifferent to him. "I am rarely disappointed in you, my dear," he said, forgetting their company for the moment.

"Come then, we will take a stroll outdoors and you may tell me your news." He took her elbow and they walked out the back door towards the gardens.

At their backs, Cookie and Mrs. Baxley exchanged knowing glances. Cookie sighed. "It won't do, you know."

"Aye, then, and it isn't the difference in their ages, but, the spread in their natures." Mrs. Baxley shrugged.

"I've got to tell ye, dear, it do worrit me at times."

"Does it, m'lovey. Well, never mind. Love will out and has a way of righting itself come what may."

Outside, Maxie took the doctor's hand, heedless of what Mrs. Baxley or Cookie might think if they were witness to such saucy behavior. She was excited beyond words as she gasped but one, soulful question. "Well, sir?"

He laughed, "It has exceeded your publisher's expectations. Yes, it is going into another printing. Mr. Evans forwarded your first royalty voucher and it is quite sizeable. I took the liberty of depositing it to your account." His smile faded and was replaced by a frown. "For the moment your secret is safe, but, it may prove difficult to continue this for any length of time. In addition to the problem of banking your funds without anyone growing suspicious, there is Evans. Maxie, he wants me to give an interview to the *Chronicle*. I feel like a cad, lying to him, taking credit for *your* work. It grows so complicated."

She touched his hands. "You are not a cad, dear, dear sir. You are doing me the favor of lending me your name. I could not publish under my own. It would utterly ruin my chances for marriage, or so my aunt says. I would be labeled a blue-stocking if it ever got out that I enjoy writing."

"Yes, indeed I do, but—"

"There are no buts involved here, Dr. John, and as to the banking, perhaps, I should open an account in London. You could then relay the funds through my solicitor. Well, I don't have one, but, I suppose I could engage one, could I not?"

He smiled ruefully. "You have quite a mind, my child—"

She cut him off with a darkling look, "And that is another thing. *I* am not a child. I am eighteen . . . nearly nineteen. One day soon I shall leave the protection of my uncle's house and set up an establishment of my own."

The good doctor laughed, caught Maxine's warning look and cut himself off. "But, Maxine, you can not be serious?"

"Why not?" Her fine dark brow was up as was her well-shaped chin.

"You should not be entertaining such outrageous notions. Depend upon it, you will find yourself engaged to be married before the year is out."

"Oh, I rather think not," scoffed Maxine. "At least not while my aunt is busy launching poor Claire." There was no bitterness in her voice. It was just a matter of fact that she had long ago accustomed herself to accepting.

"Nonsense. It is your aunt's duty to bring you out. After all you are certainly old enough and she can not very well launch Claire and not you."

Maxine shrugged. "It doesn't matter. I don't have any sort of dowry to speak of. At least, I didn't, and I can't very well tell my aunt and uncle about the remunerations I have received without giving away my secret."

"As to that, a man in love would not weigh the question of a dowry."

Maxine was obliged to laugh. Her disposition was romantic, but it rarely clouded her good-sense. "Oh, now who is speaking nonsense?"

"Maxine, you must realize what a beautiful young lady you are. You must know that in spite of the lack of dowry you think is so important, you are a most desirable young woman."

Maxine blushed at the sound of the compliment. She had not received too many of them in the years following the untimely death of her parents. "Doctor John, you have quite made my day. How very kind you always are."

"My dear, it has nought to do with kindness."

They were interrupted at this point by the sound of a horse's shoes scrapping stones and looked up to find

Freddy bearing down on them. "Hallo, how are you, sir? Thought I'd find you here Maxie-girl!"

"Did you, by faith?" Max smiled, her hands going to her hips. "And why then did you feel you must run me to earth?"

Freddy spluttered. "Didn't. Papa sent me to fetch you. Said if we hurried, we might help him choose his new hunter. He is on his way over to Tat's Farm to have a look at the new arrivals from Devon."

"Really?" She turned to the doctor, "Well then, dear sir. I am off." She gave him her hand and this time he put her ungloved fingers to his lips. It was something he had never done before. Their eyes met and Maxine felt herself blushing hotly. This was something new, something unexpected. She liked things just the way they were. She wasn't ready for anything different, anything that made her feel uncomfortable and suddenly she felt shy. She looked away and moved towards the paddock where her horse was happily grazing.

The doctor sensed only that she was shy and this pleased him. He turned amiably towards Freddy. "Well then, Frederick, soon off for university life?"

Freddy was about to turn seventeen. He had been accepted at Cambridge, but, his inclination was not studious. He loved his father's lands. He loved being about, watching the smooth running of farmland that would one day be his own. Neither his mother nor his father seemed inclined to push him, and he hoped they would agree that he had no need of more education. He frowned at the doctor, ready for a debate because he knew that the doctor would take Maxine's part, and Maxine wanted him to go to university.

"Not interested. Rather tend my father's lands and hunt with the Romney Hounds."

Maxine had led her horse to the fence where her tack rested and swung the dark brown saddle with it's worn pad onto her horse's back. "Mistake Freddy, I can't tell you enough. It is a major, major mistake."

The doctor saw that she was too quick for him and had already managed to saddle her horse. He sighed and turned to Freddy once more. "Maxine is right there."

"My parents agree with *me* and uphold my decision in this," he said, the irritation showing in his tone.

"Your parents enjoy having you home. They don't realize just what you are about," Maxine said.

The doctor looked from Maxine to Freddy for a long moment. What was this? Was the lad getting into trouble? He would have to talk to Maxine about it at another time.

Freddy could scarcely contain himself. As soon as he and Maxine trotted out of earshot he turned in his saddle to frown at his cousin. "I wish you would stop hounding me about Cambridge. I know your opinion for pity's sake!"

"Someone has to try and talk sense into you, Freddy. I know you, better than anyone else does. We have been through one or two adventures together, and I rather think you are playing too deep this time. I have ap-

pointed myself to the job of watching out for you."
Maxie answered easily, not in the least daunted by his
scowling face.

He attempted to glare at her another minute or so,
but, Maxie would not back down. She knew her powers
and her limitations. He loved her, almost as much as she
loved him. He was a brother to her, and they had always been close.

He gave up the battle and took on a whining note,
"Max, give over do."

"Freddy, you are so lucky. You are a man. You have
funds enough to enjoy an academic life, perhaps even
travel abroad and acquire town polish if you like. It just
is not the thing for you to go on larking about here with
Captain Toby."

"Max, you know Toby is a friend, thought he was
yours as well. Seems to me, we spent many an afternoon
on his boat." He shook his head at her. "As to Cambridge, even Papa only spent one year there before he
came home to run Huntly Grange."

"Your poor papa had no choice. He came down to
take care of a faltering estate when his own father died,"
snapped Maxie much annoyed that she had to bother
reminding Freddy of this. "And your father did not go
about with a known smuggler, and as much as I like
Captain Toby, that is what he is!"

"Dash it, Max! That isn't fair. Toby isn't a smuggler.
He is a fisherman." He eyed her for a moment. "You
shouldn't be saying such things."

"What then? Do you take me for a green girl? I am
no prissy miss, as you well know. I know these marshes

as well as you do, if not better. Even in the dark, I am not blind or deaf to the things that have been going bump in the night. I know what an owler is my buck!"

Freddy went white. His Max was just too smart. She knew, maybe not all, but, she knew something. He stalled her with a rueful smile, "I dessay you do know what an owler is, as do I. Still, it has little to do with either of us."

"Does it Freddy? Good, because the real truth is this. If such people did have something to do with you, it would involve the entire family, would it not?"

Freddy blushed, then urged his horse into a canter, refusing to answer Max.

Chapter Six

Lord Waremont eyed his friend, Kinnaid, as Peltons led them toward the drawing room door, where the family had gathered to await their arrival. Kinnaid returned the look warily and whispered a desperate, "What?"

"Oh, I was just wondering where the good Mrs. Huntly would seat you tonight?"

"You weren't wondering old boy. You know very well where she means to seat me. She thinks I am Waremont the great, Waremont the rich, and means to sell off her daughter to me if she can." Sir Leigh sounded disgusted.

"Don't have the stomach for it, do you my lad?" Waremont's blue eyes twinkled mischievously. "See now, that is where we differ. You allow the shallow souls of our manipulative society to blue-devil you. I allow them to amuse me."

"The thing is, her daughter, well, Seth . . . she seems so very embarrassed by her mother's machinations?"

"Ah, careful now, the seemingly sweet and innocent

are rarely so. Just look, my boy, from whence she came."

Kinnaid frowned over the problem. In truth, of course Seth was in the right of it. He sighed. "It is just so disheartening to think that a mother would push her daughter to chase after a man simply because of his rank and fortune."

"Ah, but the prize, my changeling, the prize when at hand is such temptation." Waremont chuckled.

"Now you are doing it too brown. I tell you what though, Seth, I'll be glad when we are well out of this game. Damn, but there isn't any sport in it."

"No? I don't agree. I have been enjoying myself immensely."

Peltons had opened the door and had resonantly announced their names. Kinnaid (as Waremont) took the lead and entered the room.

Kinnaid feeling far more guilty than he had admitted to Lord Waremont, went first to Mrs. Huntly to bring her proffered hand to his lips. He was diverted from this, however, by the insistent intrusion of a lively young man who stood before him determined to blind him with his bright smile. Freddy's mother glared at him, and attempted to wave him off with a flick of her hand, but, Freddy would not be put off. He had, since his initial introduction to both Waremont and Sir Leigh, discovered that these were not mere mortals, but Corinthians of the first stare! In addition to that, a tale had been recounted to him about Waremont's riding prowess that he wanted to confirm. Youthful exuberance won out over gentle manners!

"I say, my lord"—Freddy stuck in as his mother paused to take breath—"is it true that you raced Lord Beaumont to Brighton last month and set a new record?"

"Frederick," said his mother icily, "please don't bother his lordship with such absurdities."

Kinnaid controlled the urge to squirm. Of course, Waremont had run such a race. How could he take the credit? Well, but, he was posing as Waremont. He must take the credit. Complicated. This was getting a sight too complicated. He smiled at Mrs. Huntly and quietly said, "I don't mind." Then turning to Freddy, he managed a patient nod of the head. "Indeed, a new record was set."

"Famous! Did you use that bay you were riding today and yesterday?"

"No. That was a big grey stallion who is, at the moment, residing happily at Waremont in the Cotswolds."

"Claire, darling?" said Mrs. Huntly suddenly drawing attention to her daughter and away from her son, "I am sure our guests would like some of that excellent brandy your father keeps on the sideboard. Why don't you do the honors tonight my love." Pure surprise showed itself in Claire's grey eyes for this was a duty usually relegated to her father, however, she could see that he was involved in a hearty discussion with Sir Leigh. She got to her feet and moved to the dark gothic-styled wall table, saying lightly, "Of course, Mother, I should be delighted."

Kinnaid watched her get up and it occurred to him that she was certainly an elegant creature. "Here, allow me to help you with that," he offered quickly in an effort to be away from Mrs. Huntly and Frederick's youthful curiosity. Claire offered him a soft smile and said sweetly, "That would be very nice, my lord."

During this time, Maxie, dressed in another of Claire's gowns, had been watching the entire company with great interest, but, especially, Sir Leigh. She could not help but compare him with Lord Waremont. They seemed very, very different from one another. Here was Sir Leigh, new owner of Romney Grange, looking more like a royal duke! There, talking easily with Claire, not a hint of rake about him was Lord Waremont. The picture did not fit the image she had received from Lady Waremont's vivid descriptions of her son.

Look there, she told herself as she studied the gentleman conversing with Claire. His coat of soft grey was of modest design as was the way he tied his cravat. She sighed and returned her attention to the man calling himself, Sir Leigh. Waves of sandy colored hair framed a handsome face. His height, his wide shoulders, his exceptional style, his carriage, all depicted a self-assured pink of ton. The dark blue superfine coat. The fine diamond stickpin in the intricate folds of his cravat, his tight-fitting soft blue britches, his gleaming black Hessian boots, all spoke of fashion and money. It was so odd. Maxie moved towards the fireplace and took up the iron poker for lack of anything else to do.

The real Lord Waremont had been patiently listening to his host's homily, waiting for the moment when he could escape and wend his way toward Miss Tarnover. Freddy came to his rescue. As he enthusiastically began regaling his worthy parent with a dramatic description of his day's exploits, Lord Waremont seized the opportunity to approach Maxine.

He had discovered quite soon after their second meeting that in spite of her ingénue's appearance, this was no ordinary miss. Tonight she was looking exquisite. Her black curls framed her forehead and ears in a deliciously provocative manner. The remaining tresses were gathered at the nape of her neck with an aqua velvet ribbon that matched the color of her velvet gown. His blue eyes ran over her lovely figure as she bent over the fire. The heart-shaped bodice of the gown was trimmed with delicate white lace, as were the cuffs of the tight-fitting long sleeves. The waist was fitted to her own very small one and then flowed neatly over her trim hips. She certainly looked a picture.

"Here allow me to do that for you." Waremont said softly. She was a lovely female, why not enjoy a mild flirtation?

"Don't you think a female can manage a fire properly?" Maxine riposted, her ready smile uplifted to his handsome face. He saw the tease in her violet eyes and his own blue twinkled as he answered, "On the contrary, Miss Tarnover, I think a female dangerously capable of starting a fire. Controlling it? Hmmm, well now, that is a very different story?"

Maxie blushed. Now *here* was a London beau, probably one that was a sure heart-breaker. Well, she knew better than to allow such a fellow to tie her in knots! "You may find, should you get to know me, that control is not something I lack." She did not know why her knees were shaking, but managed to smile saucily at him all the same.

Waremont was taken aback. He had not expected her to be such a prodigious flirt. He moved in, reaching to take the poker from her and as his hand covered hers, was further surprised to feel oddly stimulated. The art of dalliance, its immediate pleasures, its limited goals and harvests were well-learned. He had no business reacting like a schoolboy and he was greatly annoyed with himself. Give and take dalliance with a woman who knew and understood the rules need not be measured. This chit knew how to flirt with her eyes, but, she was just a green girl and he would not allow this to go too far. In a considerably cooler tone he answered her, "Ah, but, I would not like to see your lovely gown soiled by smoke."

She released the iron to him at once. It was as if it had turned red-hot. "Thank you. You are . . . so, er . . . kind." She answered, then looked toward Claire who stood by Lord Waremont.

Waremont noted her line of vision and frowned. Did she mean to set her cap at fame and fortune? Was she like all the rest? The notion was disturbing. She had not appeared to be made of such stuff. Aye, and when did he set the least store by appearances? Females were very wonderful artists when it came to appearances.

Maxine turned to find blue eyes appraising her thoughtfully and was struck by the frown in the handsome face. "What is it, Sir Leigh?" she asked, "What is wrong?"

They were interrupted at that moment by Claire who smiled as she approached, "La, I feel a fool. Here is your brandy, good sir. I have been holding it for you all this time, but—"

"No, the fault was mine," stuck in Kinnaid as he joined them and raised his own snifter of brandy to his friend. "I am afraid I kept Miss Huntly from her course."

"I was too well entertained to notice that you two were keeping my brandy from me," said Waremont with a genuine smile.

Kinnaid sipped at the dark wine and pronounced, "Well, this is a very fine brew."

Mr. Huntly winked as he approached them. "Aye, the best that France has to offer."

"And we know better than to ask how you come by it in such troubled times," said Waremont lightly, though his blue eyes noted Maxine's frown.

Freddy leaned into Maxie and whispered, "You see, even Papa is not offended by the gentlemen."

"The *gentlemen* as you call them are not so. They are flaskers, or as I see them, smugglers," she hissed on a low note.

"You don't approve?" Lord Waremont had overheard her and his blue eyes watched the guarded look that passed between her and Frederick Huntly.

"It isn't a question of my approving or not. There are those who feel they have no choice. They take their chances and now and then pay the consequences. I simply object to giving them romantic names such as the gentlemen," returned Maxine attempting to inaugurate another facet of the topic and thus, lead them away from the heart of the matter.

"But, Max," objected Freddy.

His father put up a hand, "Maxine is quite right. They are a pack of scoundrels every last one, though they serve a purpose. Can't get the two notions confused, Freddy-lad."

"No, Papa, they are not scoundrels. At least no more than we are. They smuggle the brandy, we drink it—"

"That is enough!" snapped Mr. Huntly who was not about to allow his son to compare him to a pack of smugglers.

Maxine breathed a sigh of relief when Mrs. Huntly appeared at that dangerous moment and brightly announced that their dinner was ready to be served. She was at her most cheerful as she turned to take her husband's arm and move towards the open doorway saying over her shoulder, "Oh, Claire, that's a good girl, you take his lordship's arm into dinner, that's right, and Maxine, you may bring along Sir Leigh. Freddy darling, would you fetch my shawl from the sofa? Lovely."

And with matters organized to her satisfaction, Mrs. Huntly led the way to dinner.

Chapter Seven

Waremont and Kinnaid stepped out of the bank onto the curbing and looked down the cobbled alley to the busy fishing port. There was something exciting, mysterious about Rye. This was no sleepy little fishing village, but the center of Romney Marsh. Secrets abounded and one felt their lure, their whispers on the fresh salt air.

Waremont breathed deep and grinned. "I tell you what, old boy. Glad I accompanied you on this trip!"

"Are you? Well, I was just thinking that I damned well wished you had not," returned Kinnaid gloomily.

Waremont shot him a quick appraisal. "Now that is not like you. In fact, you've been blue-deviled all morning. It is the Huntlys, right?" Waremont knew of course that his friend had come away from Huntly Grange very much the worse for wear. Kinnaid had not enjoyed the evening and had been thoroughly shaken by guilt. Waremont was feeling much the same.

"The thing is, I like Mr. Huntly, I like Miss Huntly and her brother, and I feel like a cad playing them false.

It isn't right and we were out of line," said Kinnaid his grey eyes dark with his brooding.

In truth, this was precisely what Waremont had felt as his head had touched his pillow the night before. However, they had switched their identities and it was too late now to retract. He frowned and sighed an acquiescence. "I suppose you are in the right of it, Leigh. Nothing for it now, but to stay out of the way until tis time to return to London."

"Seth . . . why Seth, darling!" exclaimed a familiar voice.

Waremont looked round to find an extremely beautiful redhead gliding across the cobbled street, her gloved hands extended towards him. "Fanny! Well, my sweet, you are certainly a sight for hungry eyes." He smiled a warm welcome. Fanny Curlew had been the latest of his intimate flirts. She had a comfortable life, bequeathed to her by her late husband (a man who had been forty years her senior). She was eight-and-twenty. She was *ton*, she knew the rules and had been an enjoyable lover. However, suddenly she had wanted more. She wanted marriage and Waremont had made the decision to quietly drift out of her realm.

She reached him and as he took her hands she managed to place a soft kiss on his mouth. She arched a pretty look to Kinnaid and pursed a kiss at him, lightly saying, "La, I never thought to find you two in Rye?" She linked her arm through his. "What are you doing here?"

"We might ask you the same question."

"La, but you must recall me mention my dear aunt

Sarah? The one who is richer than a nabob? She has
not been well, poor dear." She smiled without warmth.
"I am her favorite ... her only niece. She was never
married and has no children. I thought it was time I visited her. She has a lovely house just outside of the village."

"How very wise of you," said Kinnaid. He did not
like Fanny and made little secret of this. He thought her
scheming, cunning and cold-hearted and he had been
happy to see Waremont out of her clutches.

"La, but as ever, you are so very sweet, are you not,
Sir Leigh?" Fanny returned her attention to Waremont.
"Darling, you, on the other hand, have not been sweet
at all, have you?"

"Then I have been abominably remiss and you
should chastise me severely," he answered her softly. He
had no intention of picking up where they had left off,
but he would maintain a friendship if he could.

Maxine had gone into Rye and had been enjoying
herself immensely at the milliners. Loaded with hat-
boxes, she came outdoors and saw across the cobbled
street Kinnaid, Waremont and an exquisitely beautiful
redhead with the look of London in her style.

Waremont's blue eyes glanced across the street at that
same moment. There stood Max. She looked adorable
in her yellow spencer. Her black curls peeped beneath
her straw bonnet and she raised her hand in greeting.
Hurriedly he looked away. He took up Fanny's elbow

whispering to his friend in an aside as he steered them off, "Leigh . . . don't look, just come along."

Kinnaid knew, sensed that there was someone they were avoiding and so great was his fear of being discovered by the Huntlys that he obeyed without question. Fanny was pleased to go anywhere with his lordship, and did so chattering happily all the while.

Max was momentarily stunned by his bad manners. At least, his friend, Waremont had not seen her and thus, must be excused. What? Did Sir Leigh Kinnaid think she might actually walk over and interrupt his tête â tête with the redhead? Maxine felt her cheeks go hot. Well, of all the rude, arrogant, self-centered, egotistical men she had ever come across, this one reigned supreme!

This was not what she had expected of him. Last night he had been disposed to be pleasant. He had directed his conversation at her and she had admitted to herself that in spite of his arrogance, he was certainly charming. Charming? Ha! He was a *jackanape!*

Feeling suddenly depressed, she untethered her carriage horse and climbed onto the seat of her open gig. Sighing heavily, she sat a moment, lost to her blistering thoughts before clucking to her cob and giving the reins a flick of the wrists to move her horse forward.

It did not take her long to get home, leave the cob and the gig to the groom, and carry her band-boxes to her room. Once there she sulked a moment as she plopped on her bed. However, she was soon throwing off her lovely new gown and slipping into her comfortable boy's britches and walking boots. She threw on her favorite buckskin short-coat. She needed to walk!

She took the backstairs, thus, avoiding any chance meeting with any family member and made a quick stop in the kitchen. There she wrapped a loaf of bread in a napkin.

Cook raised an eyebrow but, shook her head and smiled, "Go on, go on before I see whot yer doing."

It was a wonderful day for walking. The breeze felt refreshing against her cheeks hot still from her tickled temper. She took the wooded path away from the house that led to the river Rother and walked along its banks until she came to the dock her uncle had commissioned local carpenters to build some years ago. There she sat and looked out on the river's artful winding path, until she saw him. Maxie smiled to herself and called out, "Well, there you are Cyg!" The young swan turned and Maxie threw out a piece of bread and waited for the young swan to approach. She bent to meet him as he came close and urged him closer still. "Come then . . . that's my boy."

The swan was no more than six, perhaps seven months old. He had been chased off by his family, and arrived on the embankment, his neck badly injured. Freddy and Max had been enjoying a day's fishing when they noticed him and both had taken instant pity. He had been too weak to fight Max when she tended to his wound, and too happy for the scraps of food they had given him from their luncheon basket. The following weeks both Freddy and Max had spent a great deal of time tending to him. That had been just about the beginning of August, some five weeks ago. His white down was still sprinkled with soft brown, and the feathers were starting to grow in and cover his scars at his young neck.

He came up close now and took the proffered bread from her fingers and Max examined his neck. "Well now, my lad, you are looking much better. In no time at all you shall have new feathers growing in."

Waremont had managed to escape Fanny some moments after he and Kinnaid were out of Maxine's sight. They took to horse and rode out of Rye. They had left the clang of the cobblestones for the sandy country lane that would take them to Romney Grange when Kinnaid turned a frown to ask, "Dash it, Seth! What the devil was all that about?"

"What, Fanny? You know I am well out of that, but, no need to give the lady a set-down."

"Confound you! I'm not talking about Fanny. Don't give a fig about Fanny and she is too thick-skinned to notice if you did. Why didn't you want me to look across the street? Who were we avoiding?"

"Miss Maxine Tarnover." Waremont had been in a strange mood since he had seen her and ignored her greeting. He felt a cad. In fact, he could not recall ever feeling so despicable about anything ever before. What could she be thinking about him?

"Deuce take it! Did she see us?"

"She did. She waved," said Waremont gravely.

"Blister it! Upon my soul! Never say so, Seth."

"I am afraid I snubbed the young lady, and there is no need to go on about it, Leigh. I feel hipped enough as it is."

"Aye, we've gone and done it this time, haven't we old boy? It is as much my fault as yours. I agreed to play the game, didn't I?"

The two covered the distance to Romney Grange without speaking a word, but as Kinnaid began to dismount, Waremont said quietly, "Go on then, Leigh, I need to ride."

The river Rother flowed easily through Romney Grange lands, dipped through Huntly Grange as well before it linked the village of Rye to the sea. Waremont rode towards the river, taking a wooded path along its winding course. He found he was more distressed with his behavior than he was willing to admit. He had little respect for Mrs. Huntly. She was after all, playing her own game, wasn't she? Indeed, she certainly was. However, he had found that her husband was a good and honest man. As to their daughter, she seemed a nice enough miss, only doing as her mother bid. A weak girl. He liked Freddy and thought him a decent lad. That left only Maxine. What exactly was Maxine? All minx one moment, innocent hoyden, and then a saucy woman would suddenly emerge. He had not liked to see the hurt on her face when he had snubbed her earlier in town. She would not understand that sort of behavior. How could he explain it to her? It had been unforgivable. He slowed his horse to a walk, and realized that he had taken a direction that had put him at Huntly Grange. Perhaps, he would call on Miss Tarnover and try to repair the damage? No, that would be a bacon-brained thing to do. And then he saw her!

She was leaning over the dock towards a young swan, hand-feeding it, and her long black hair was in perfect disarray around her pretty profile. She looked like a beautiful child, innocent and unassuming in her boy's clothing.

Suddenly she got to her feet, looking very frightened as she ran along the embankment and shouted something he could not hear. What was wrong? What had disturbed the peace of the moment? He looked past the young swan and saw them, two adult swans with three of their brood. The adult swans had spanned their wings and puffed themselves up to do battle. Their necks were crooked as they stalked their helpless prey. Cyg saw them coming and began to peep in terrified accents. He was a creature of the wild, but, as Maxie called to him, he glided towards her as though seeking her protection.

Waremont instinctively jumped off his horse. He tethered the gelding to a nearby tree and moved to Maxie's side. She was gathering rocks and throwing them at the adult swans. This seemed to startle them for a moment and they bent their necks to have a look at Maxine and Waremont. Cyg used the moment to swim close to Max and dive his long neck between a piling and the bulwarks. Maxie looked to Waremont for help, giving him a large rock and saying breathlessly, "I think they mean to kill him if they can. These must have been the ones who injured him before, my poor Cyg!" She looked up desperately. "Please, help me?"

Suddenly, the mother swan had Cyg's neck and he

screeched out in pain. Maxie cried out pitifully and moved toward the river. She looked as though she meant to throw herself between them and physically stop the attack on the young swan. Waremont heaved the rock hard and it landed near the mother swan's chest. She backed off hissing all the while. Whimpering, Cyg attempted to squeeze his body behind the piling. Waremont could see that these adult swans would not give this up for already mother swan was returning in spite of their presence. With ready determination, Waremont went to his knees and bent down. He quickly took hold of Cyg's neck and tail. In a flash he had him out of the water. He carried Cyg to the grass away from the dock and the river's edge. Placing the swan gently down, Waremont shook his head and said softly, "There lad, you'll do."

Mother and father swan did not seem deterred by this and remained near the water's edge hissing as they looked toward Cyg. He took a few awkward steps away, planted himself, and began to preen at his feathers, content to be out of harm's way. Maxie hurled abuse and rocks at his attackers, reproving them severely for their cruel and unnatural behavior. Waremont stood a long moment watching her before going to her side. He took up a few rocks and hurled them towards the adult swans until at last, mother and father gathered their remaining children and glided further down the river. Maxie turned and saw poor Cyg's wound had been reopened.

"Oh no, look what they have done! And after it was healing so nicely?" She fought back the tears that sprang into her violet eyes, and shook her head. "Poor little fellow."

"The salt water will take care of that," Waremont said softly, assuagingly.

Maxine regarded him. When he had arrived on the scene, there hadn't been a moment to think. She had needed help and he had not scoffed off her concerns. If he had not handled the situation so well, poor Cyg would have been injured all the more. Of this fact, she was quite certain. Though Cyg was only seven months old, he weighed a great deal more than she would have been able to carry out of the river as easily as Waremont had done. His gentleness with the young swan surprised her. She glanced at him now, pure gratitude in her violet eyes. "Thank you, Sir Leigh. You were more than wonderful. You were poor Cyg's hero!"

"Nonsense. You were doing very well without me." He smiled at her.

"No . . . I was not . . ." She shook her head. "I can't thank you enough."

"Oh, but, your young swan was in no danger while you were on watch. Tell me, would you have actually jumped into the river?"

She looked sheepish for a moment. "I didn't know what else to do. I would not have been able to carry him out as you did."

"Once in the river, just what would you have done?" He was scanning her features and it occurred to him that he had never known any female like to this one.

She grinned. "Well, being a girl, I'm not handy with m'fives as Freddy would say, but, I think I might have startled them enough to keep them at bay. However, I might have frightened Cyg into the open. I don't think he can fly yet, and he can't out-swim them and at this particular spot on the river there is little room for escape."

"Remarkable," he said. He was looking into her eyes and noted a warm light in their violet hue that was most enchanting. He saw something else. He saw doubt. She was wondering still about his behavior towards her in town. What could he say? Nought. If she ignored it, he would take her cue.

Maxine rarely ignored anything. It was not her way. She was direct to a fault. "Lucky for me . . . for Cyg that you came along. I suppose you were on your way home from town?" She knew very well that this was not so. How could it be when he was on Huntly lands?

He eyed her. "In a manner of speaking, I suppose I was." He answered briefly, ignoring her inquiring eyes.

"I was in town myself this morning," she continued. There was the bait. Would he bite?

"Yes, I know."

"I rather thought you did," she answered, and moved away from him. What could she do? Who was this man? One minute he had been a hero, helping her, getting himself soiled by bird and dirt. The next moment he was the man who had arrogantly snubbed her in town. Why had he done that? Why did he not offer an explanation? What was he made of?

"Oh!" Maxie exclaimed suddenly distracted by Cyg who had decided it was time to return to the river. She moved in on him and began clucking and cooing, throwing him bits of bread. Cyg picked at a chunk of bread, ignored the rest and wobbled disjointedly to the embankment's edge.

Cyg began peeping wildly as there was no easy access to the river. Maxine looked to Waremont. Her violet eyes were intense as she said, "He can't get back to the water from here."

"I suppose I am on duty again?" laughed Waremont.

Sweetly she lowered her violet eyes and then raised them to his blue. "Please, Sir Leigh ... if you ... could?"

Cautiously he approached Cyg who eyed him warily and began to warn him off with a hiss. Observing that this human was intent on his purpose, Cyg attempted to run, but a swan's movements on land are cumbersome and Waremont soon had him once more by neck and tail. He brought him to the dock and bent as low as he could so that when he dropped Cyg, he landed quite nicely on his belly. Cyg wiggled his tail and ducked his sore neck, gulped at the water and moved off toward the estuary.

Waremont and Maxie watched him vanish round the bend and then turned to one another. Maxie held out her hand. "Thank you."

"Wait ... I think I am now entitled to hear about Cyg—for cygnet, I assume—don't you?" He had enjoyed this interlude with her and the swan. He wasn't ready to go back to Kinnaid's predictions of doom and gloom.

She smiled almost shyly at him. "Indeed, you are, Sir Leigh, but I am overdue and must hurry home and change these clothes before my aunt sees me." With a giggle and a wave she was off.

Waremont stood a long moment looking after her. She was certainly a charming little hoyden!

Chapter Eight

Toby was a large man with a swarthy sun-tanned face. He moved with a peculiar grace for such a big fellow as he tended the rigging of his fishing boat. The day had not been one of his better ones, but, he was not complaining. No, not he! He was the son of a Devonshire cobbler and would always have his father's trade to fall back on should things become too risky at sea. The unhappy truth was, he was bound to the sea by love. He had an urgent need to wield his vessel through its rough, wild, and mysterious waters. He was a sorry cobbler, but an exceptional sailor. The thought of giving it up blue-deviled him. Damn, but, fishing was scarcely making him a living and though the money was good in other quarters, it was getting to be a sight too dangerous these days!

"Toby!" Freddy called out as Toby disembarked onto the busy dock, "All done for the day?"

"Aye and I be wondering whot ye be doing 'ere so late in the day?" Toby's hazel eyes surveyed the young man ruefully.

"Tob, it isn't that late." Freddy grimaced as he fell in step beside the large man.

"Don't be pitching yer gammon at me halflin'! They'll be looking for ye at 'ome before long and well ye know it. Ye jest don't care." Toby bent to pat the collie at Freddy's side. Melody wagged her tail vigorously in reception. "Don't want no fingers pointed this way, lad . . . are we clear on that?"

"Aye then Toby." Freddy grinned. "I'll just walk with you towards the Mermaid and then be on my way."

Doctor John Wiltshire saw the last of his supplies loaded into his cart. It was deuced inconvenient having to do these things for himself. Well, there was just so much money a country doctor could make. All he could afford outside his cook and his housekeeper was one manservant, and that one man could not be expected to do everything. He sighed over the problem.

Dreaming of better days, he looked up and noticed Frederick Huntly across the cobbled avenue, walking the dockside with a man who was rather well known in Rye, Captain Toby. This was not the first time he had noticed young Frederick in the company of a man the excise officers called the Devil of the Deep. It was most troublesome. Oh, it was true that there was no proof that Toby was a smuggler. No one had ever caught him in the act, though they tried. In fact, it was a source of amazement to Doctor John that the smugglers managed to perfect their art while the revenuers had an infinite capacity to fail in their efforts to catch the gentlemen.

It was a source of concern that Frederick was so often to be found in Toby's company. If the lad did not discontinue his thoughtless, irresponsible larking, he would involve his family in an ugly scandal. Doctor John had every hope of being united in marriage to the Huntly family, and found such a possibility most disturbing.

He consulted his pocket watch and decided that perhaps the hour was not yet too advanced to swing by Huntly Grange on his way home and pay Maxine a call. It might be wise to drop a whisper into Maxie's pretty ear. She seemed to exert some influence with the boy. At any rate, he wanted to visit with her and pay his respects to the family. It was time.

Claire was taking a stroll about the grounds. Her head was in a muddle and she needed to clear her mind. She needed to walk, think things out. Everything was suddenly so confusing.

Until yesterday evening she had thought herself falling in love with Doctor John Wiltshire. Doctor John was so sweet, so charming, so suitable. There too, he was forever at the Grange and their friendship seemed to be developing into something much more. Then out of nowhere, the man she knew as Lord Waremont had arrived to shake up her easy complacent world.

Lord Waremont was everything any woman could ever want in a man. He was so very attractive in his modest, unobtrusive manner. He was clever, he was gentle, he was very sweet, and had such warm grey eyes so full with ready understanding. She was of course, thinking like a silly goose. He would soon be off for London and think no more about her!

The sound of cart wheels on the driveway brought her head round to find Doctor John driving up towards her. She smiled and waved a welcome. Here was Doctor John, so dear, so pleasant. She frowned and chastised herself for being no more than a fickle ninny!

Doctor John pulled up his cart just short of the Huntly stable, set the brake in place, jumped hurriedly to the ground and smiled warmly towards Claire as he handed the reins to a young stable lad. In a quiet, but authoritative, voice he requested the boy to tend to his horse, though he would only be a few minutes.

As Claire approached him, he noted that she was looking quite pretty in her walking ensemble of emerald green. She did not have Maxine's provocative sensuality, but she certainly was an attractive young woman. She held out her kid gloved hand to him and he brought her dainty fingers to his lips, allowing his eyes to smile into hers as he greeted her. "Miss Claire, lovely as ever."

She smiled sweetly at him. Claire was not a flirt by nature, however, she certainly was enjoying the attention. "How nice to see you, Doctor John. Won't you come up to the house and have some ale?"

"Indeed, I should like that very much." He wondered if Maxine were indoors.

* * *

Maxine was at that moment scurrying along the wooded path, past the stables. She saw Doctor John's cart and peeped round the stable building in time to watch him kiss Claire's gloved fingers. Well, well, she smiled to herself, just what do we have here? A romance in the making? This did not really surprise her, for she had been thinking that Claire was interested in Doctor John.

She started off once more for the house, but, Doctor John spotted her and called out, "Maxie!"

Maxie turned round, a guilty expression flitting over her features. Caught, nothing for it. "Oh, hallo, you two."

Claire looked darkly at Max and pulled a face, "Maxine," she chided, "Why must you wear such clothes in public?"

"Well, what would be the sense in wearing them in private?" Max giggled. "Besides, Cyg likes my britches."

"Oh, that swan again." Claire smiled affectionately. "Is he well?"

"Claire, something awful happened, but, Sir Leigh came along and set everything to rights." She smiled at the doctor, "You must recall my mentioning our young swan?"

"Ah, yes."

"Well, his parents came back today and wanted to kill him," said Maxine in horrified accents.

"Never say so." Claire's hands went to her cheeks. "Oh, poor thing."

"I take it they were not successful," pursued the doctor for he wanted to hear more about this Sir Leigh.

"No, they were not. I threw rocks at them, though it

didn't help overly, but then, Sir Leigh just went in and scooped Cyg up which wasn't as easy as it sounds because Cyg is heavy and he put up a struggle. Sir Leigh managed him very nicely and then made short work of frightening off poor Cyg's attackers." She smiled apologetically at the doctor, "However, I now must try and get to my room without my aunt catching me in britches again." She looked to Claire. "You, I am persuaded, understand my anxiety to be off?"

"Yes, yes, of course Maxine." Claire touched her arm, "Go on then, for I think mama is in her bedchamber."

"I, on the other hand, do not enjoy being left with only half a story. I should like to hear the remainder of this tale ... perhaps, some day when you are properly dressed?" The tease was bright in Doctor John's hazel eyes.

She laughed, "Agreed! Well, that is, I shall be happy to relate all the details of my swan's adventure today, but, I promise nothing about how I shall be dressed!" So saying she waved herself off and vanished behind the stable once more as she made her way towards the rear entrance to the house.

Claire turned a thoughtful expression to the doctor. She had not realized just how close Maxine and the doctor had become? A touch of natural jealousy moved her to say, "My cousin is very dear, but, such a child still . . ."

Doctor John merely smiled, pulled out his pocket watch and exclaimed regretfully, "I can hardly believe it is so very late already. I don't know what I have done with the day. Forgive me, dear Miss Claire. I had better be on my way." He took her hands and squeezed them, "I can't tell you how much I enjoyed being here ... with you."

Much mollified, Claire inclined her head and watched him return to his wagon. He turned to wave once more and she allowed him a slight wiggle of her fingers before she turned for the house. She rather thought she would go and have a talk with Maxine!

Freddy ducked behind a large yew tree as the doctor's cart came ambling past him on the winding front drive. "Whew" he breathed a sigh of relief. Toby had told him the doctor had seen them together. Well, the doctor's presence here could only mean that he had come to report on his whereabouts to Maxine. Deuce take the fellow, he had thought him better than that! Here was Toby, right again. Toby always knew who was to be trusted. He had a sixth sense about that sort of thing and Toby did not trust Doctor John.

As Freddy slinked past the stables taking the same route Max had taken only a moment ago. It didn't take Freddy long to reach the kitchen where he put a finger to his lips for a conspiratorial silence. He scurried through the kitchen, passing cook with a sure grin and made for the backstairs. He reached Maxine's open door, looked in and noted that his sister and Max were frowning at one another. He liked Claire well enough, but had never confided in her and was not about to start now. He stood for a moment feeling uneasy and was thankful when Claire broke the awkwardness of the moment to say, "No doubt, you two would like to exchange reports on your respective adventures of the day." Then she turned her shoulder on Max, swept past her brother and left the room.

Freddy looked after her for a moment, decided that women in the ordinary sense were strange, unfathomable creatures. He shrugged this concern off and as he closed Maxine's door asked idly, "Now, what has Miss Prim so dashed hipped?" Then shaking his head he said, "Never mind, I don't really want to know." He eyed Maxie thoughtfully and said lightly, "I saw Doctor John leaving just now."

"Did you?" returned Max absently.

Oh, oh, he thought, he was in for it now. The doctor had told her. He threw up his hands, "Look, Maxine, I don't see where the harm is if I want to spend a little time with Toby. He is a friend, after all."

"Oh, Freddy, you were with Toby today again?"

"Well, yes, but just for a bit. He would have it that it won't do for me to be forever at his side."

"Toby is right."

"Don't see that. Max, he is a capital fellow."

"Freddy, you don't understand. I like Toby. Honestly, I do, but, the thing is, one day he will be caught for the crime of smuggling and make no mistake, it is a crime against our country. We are at war with France. Smuggling—"

"He doesn't smuggle in French goods," objected Freddy lamely.

"I am not going to quibble with you. Smuggling, whether it is *wool* out of England, or wine and brandy into England, is smuggling. In the end your name will be bandied about with his. It won't do. Do you understand at least that much?"

"Aye, but, Max, he won't get caught. They have tried over and over, to no avail. He is too clever for them!" Freddy beamed proudly.

She sighed. "I hope not, Freddy-boy, because I do like him."

"I knew you did," said Freddy grinning, "You've always been a right'un, Max."

Maxie stared at him for a long moment. How was she going to handle this very sticky problem? Freddy just could not be made to understand. She just couldn't give it up. There was too much at stake, "Freddy, only do consider this; you like Toby, I like Toby and the life he leads is his own. However, we can't lead his life. We have ours to maintain. We have people other than ourselves to think about."

"I'm not doing anything wrong, Max. I'm not smuggling." Freddy looked at her.

"Look here, my bucko, maybe you didn't load the contraband onto his boat, but you gave him permission to use our dock on the river, and don't try and deny it for I was there."

"You were spying on me?" He accused her in fulminating tones.

"No, my lad. I was there for Cyg. It was in his early days when his wounds were still raw. I couldn't sleep and went down to the dock to see if he was about. I saw instead Toby's rig, I saw the owlers loading Toby's boat with their wool. Freddy, I saw *you.*" There it was out.

"What then, do you mean to tell m'father?"

Max answered him with a sad shake of her head. "Not if I think you are well out of it."

"I am, I swear it Max, he was in trouble, it was only that one time."

Maxie took Freddy's shoulders in her small hands. "Listen to me, lad, and the devil fly away with chasing up a lark, for this is not a game. The time has come to whip up your horses and pull out."

"Aye, then Max, you've no need to be in a lively dread that I shall forget what I owe my name. It is settled then."

She looked at him and wondered if he was now pitching his gammon at her as he did to the other members of his family. "I hope so, Freddy, I do really hope so," she answered him softly.

Chapter Nine

The morning was a glorious promise of autumn at its best. The earth was dressed in bright sunlight. A soft fresh breeze invited man outdoors. Everything was geared for perfection. However, the two gentlemen having breakfast together seemed steeped in gloom.

Waremont chewed moodily on a piece of very fine breakfast ham and shot a look at his friend's countenance. "You look as if you have fretted yourself to flinders all night."

"Oh, do I?" returned Kinnaid sardonically. "You, I suppose, slept like a baby?"

"As a matter of fact, no, I did not sleep well. Thank you," retorted Waremont eyeing him darkly.

"Well, here we are then, a virulent pair, the two of us . . . and with no way out."

"The devil fly away with you, Leigh. This has gone beyond bearing!" snapped Waremont. "If your conscience is eating at you so very sorely, you know very well that throwing blame around is no way out!"

"I am not blaming you. Well, I am, but, I blame myself as well. You can't help being what you are. I'm your friend. I should have known better. I should have put a stop to it, protected the both of us from our demons." Kinnaid moaned dramatically.

"The point is you didn't stop me. And probably could not have at any rate. So moaning about it now does little good."

"The thing is, I'm in lively dread of being found out and even so, I would like nothing more than to pay a morning call on the Huntlys. It is madness."

"I must confess to similar feelings. I tell you what Kinnaid, the sooner we depart for London, the better off we shall be," said Waremont thoughtfully.

"Would that we could. I have some documents being drawn up that my bailiff will need in my absence. My local solicitor hasn't finished with them yet, and there are still some papers regarding the inheritance that have to be signed." Kinnaid sighed. "Deuce take it all! I am nearly certain the Huntlys will wonder at it if we don't stop by and pay them a call while we are still at Romney. I tell you what, Seth, I feel a mongrel."

"We are in queer straits this time old boy, I'll give you that."

Maxine appraised her appearance as she gazed into the long looking glass. She could not deny, even for modesty's sake, that she loved the way her new royal blue ensemble fitted her figure. She angled the matching chip bonnet and pinched it's white and royal blue ribbons. She adjusted the white lace high collar of her bodice. She hurried across the hall to scratch at Claire's door, "Come on, are you ready?" Maxie called out merrily.

Claire opened the door and though Claire was not a giggler, she definitely giggled before she put up a graceful arm and said, "Well?" Claire was wearing an ensemble of ivory muslin trimmed in brown velvet. Maxie clapped her hands. "Beautiful. I think we make quite a pair." There had been a moment in Maxie's room yesterday, just before Frederick arrived when the two girls nearly had exchanged angry words. The moment had been interrupted and was lost during the evening, when Maxie had advised Claire that Freddy would drive them to Romney Grange in the morning. She wanted to express her thanks to Sir Leigh, by delivering to him some of Cook's best fruit tarts. She wanted him to know how very grateful she was for his help with Cyg. Claire said this was very proper and fell in with the notion with glee. Once more the girls were on the best of terms.

Freddy awaited them outdoors in the open gig. He was not adverse to visiting such Corinthians as Waremont and Sir Leigh. However, he felt the girls had certainly kept him waiting too long and was just losing patience when both girls appeared, very much in spirits and much disposed to jest and tease. Freddy fell in with this line of bantering which made the short drive to Romney Grange extremely pleasant.

* * *

Kinnaid and Waremont had just left the dining room to meander into the library. Their mood was still sombre, and their plans for the day unsettled. The library door opened and Wiggons announced in stentorian tones, "Miss Huntly, Miss Tarnover, and Mr. Frederick Huntly."

Waremont and Kinnaid exchanged wary glances. Waremont looked towards the open library door and experienced a tingle of sure anticipation. Perhaps, he told himself, this was because any diversion would have excited him? After all, he and Kinnaid had been wallowing in a crater of dullness. He felt his heart start to beat faster for as Maxie walked prettily into the room, he was sure he had never seen any woman as beautiful as she!

She went directly to him and put out her gloved hand. Her large violet eyes drew on his smile as she said, "Sir Leigh, we have brought you and Lord Waremont a basket of Cook's finest tarts. I hope you will enjoy them."

He took her gloved fingers and made a show of putting them to his lips. His blue eyes twinkled as he unbent and softly he said, "Thank you. I shall not ask how we managed to win such a treat, for you might think better of it and take it away."

He intrigued Maxie. He was a blatant contradiction of everything she was so sure of in people. One moment he was an arrogant rake, the next a gentle caring man. Just who was this wild London beau?

She could hear her cousins chatting with Waremont in the background, but, it was a buzz of noise she wanted to filter out. For the moment she wanted only to talk to this man with the twinkling blue eyes.

"Whatever I may think of you today or tomorrow, I *know* you were a hero yesterday," answered Maxie.

He laughed and inclined his head. "Ah, now that sounds as if you read gothic novels, Miss Tarnover."

"That is because I do read and enjoy them as well," she smiled amiably. "However, the truth is you saved my Cyg and I am very grateful."

He had not yet released her fingers, and now brought up her hand so that her wrist was exposed. He bent and gently placed a kiss on her wrist. She trembled and he immediately released her hand. Their eyes met and she was aware, all too aware of the electricity that suddenly shot through her entire body. Quietly, almost seductively he said, "I am very glad I was on hand to assist you."

He had stepped over Maxie's line. She controlled the urge to hide her hand behind her back. "Well, we have entered today and left yesterday behind."

He laughed and inclined his handsome head. "Touché, Miss Tarnover. I suppose I deserved that."

Ever generous she allowed him a half-smile and agreed, "Yes sir, you most certainly did."

Freddy had found Lord Waremont not at all the top sawyer, wild nobleman he had heard about. In fact, the man seemed rather tame compared to what his mental image of the fellow had been. He moved in to Max and gave her a wry smile. "Well then, have you been telling Sir Leigh about our town fair planned for this Saturday?"

It was getting so deuced tedious hearing himself

called Sir Leigh. Waremont wished there were some way of putting an end to it. Zounds! Every now and then one of his little games back-fired. In the not so distant past, youth and a tendency to be unconcerned got him through. This time, everything was different. It was as though all the rules had been changed after the game was already in progress. Leigh was right, it just wasn't the same. Damnation! He must be getting old, at least too old to be playing at such tricks. Fine then, he had surely learned a lesson. How could he set it to rights? He couldn't. Hell, and brimstone, it was too late.

He looked at Maxine. She would find his deceit inexcusable. He had never really cared overly much for the opinions of others, yet, he knew he did not want Maxine Tarnover to see him in this light. All at once he also knew that he wanted this child of a woman to know his real name. Why? Well, he told himself easily, she was not impressed with him as Sir Leigh. He wanted to impress her, bring her down a peg. That's it, that was what she needed!

Now, what was she doing? His serious cogitations had kept him gravely occupied. Maxine had been moving away from him, leaving him to Freddy's absurd chatter. She was curious about his friend, this lord so very blatantly different from his own mother's description.

She could see that he and Claire were getting on as though they had known each other forever. In fact, both Claire and this shy lord, seemed to be blushing, so heightened was the color in their cheeks.

Well, thought Waremont his blue eyes following her, just what are you doing, Miss Tarnover? Moving in on richer game? His brows came together and he found himself irritated as he only half listened to Freddy's lengthy diatribe of boyish nonsense.

"Our town fair is going to be famous good fun this Saturday," said Freddy beaming. "There will even be a cockfight! Zounds, but you will like Mr. Smith's grey. He has beaten every red for miles around. I say, Sir Leigh, are you listening?" Freddy peered up at Waremont's face.

Waremont grinned at the boy. "Indeed, Frederick, I certainly am, and I'm looking forward to seeing this cockfight. I was just thinking that we should include er . . . Lord Waremont in this outing, don't you think?"

"Aye, that I do, for it's bound to be a bang up show." agreed Freddy enthusiastically as he followed Waremont's steps toward Claire and Kinnaid.

"Here, why don't you tell his lordship all about it, while I engage to convince your cousin and sister to allow us to join your party this Saturday?"

"What is it you are at now?" asked his sister, mildly curious.

"Cockfight near the fair on Saturday," grinned Freddy happily.

"Faith, how dreadful you are," declared his sister in some disgust.

"Now, Claire, wouldn't have told you, but you would ask." Freddy sighed. "Besides, it won't interfere with your fun. You and Max can stroll about the town and buy trinkets and such while we are at the cockfight."

"You could, of course, accompany us to the cock-fight?" Waremont whispered in Maxie's ear and his blue eyes twinkled.

She pulled a face at him and whispered back, "There is no sport in watching one poor animal kill another." She eyed him challengingly. "It is a constant source of wonder to me, how it is that men must promote sports involving blood and gore—and wager on the outcome of such events?"

"Ha, there is always a sense to such things! The urge to conquer, my dear. Therein lies the lure. Men are fascinated by it. It's age-old. Did not the Romans throw humans into an arena of lions? It is in our nature."

"We have come a long way from such uncivilized behavior." Maxie frowned at him. "We are supposed to be rational, and rational beings care for weaker creatures. That is what keeps us apart from the barbarians." She shook her head. "You want a blood sport? Well then go watch men pulverize one another in the boxing ring. At least there, each player has a choice."

He smiled at her. "You make a sound argument, my girl, a sound argument." She was in earnest, he could see it, but, he meant to bait her further.

"Can it be that I have convinced you to give up betting on cockfights?" Maxine was incredulous before she was hopeful.

"No. You see, I also know that we humans rationalize what suits us and condemn what does not," he answered her softly, his blue eyes looking thoughtfully into hers. "Can you be honest, love?"

"What does that mean?" She ignored the soft caress and this new form of address.

"It is obvious. You hunt, do you not?" He lead her easily to where he wished to go. "Of course you do, as do I."

"Fox hunt? Yes, enthusiastically. Never mean to say that you wish to compare—"

He cut her off at once. "No comparison you say? And why not? It is a bloodsport m'girl, whether you want to consider it so or not."

"It is not the same thing. We perform a service. The fox wantonly destroy livestock. It doesn't even eat everything it kills. The farmers need us . . . want us . . . it is not the same thing as you suggest."

"There is your rationalization." Waremont smiled smugly. "When you are in first flight, riding to hounds, watching them hunt their prey, running the fox to earth, are you not exhilarated? The speed, the chase, the thrill of watching the hounds perform at their best. You are not thinking about the service you are doing your tenant farmers!" His voice was low, compelling and he was stating a truth. He knew it and he could see in her violet eyes that she knew it as well. She was not really fair game for there was no subterfuge in her character.

"No?" Max was frowning for she was already admitting a doubt to herself. All that he said was the sorry truth.

"Don't fret over it, sweetheart. There is no harm in it. Rational beings kill. It is inherent in our nature."

"You keep saying that." Maxie's violet eyes were

clouded over in concern. "I just can not accept such a blatant generality."

"You don't wish to. There is a vast difference," He answered glibly.

"No. Perhaps it is human nature to kill. Perhaps? However, we have something else in our nature. We have the capacity to love, to feel compassion, pity."

They were interrupted at that moment, by the appearance of a servant laden with a tray of various refreshments. Kinnaid forgot that he was playing Waremont. He forgot that it was not his home and amiably went about the business of being a good host. Maxie's brow went up.

Neither Freddy nor Claire noticed anything amiss and went on chatting happily. The servant left the room and, frowning still, Maxie turned an inquiring eye towards the blue eyes gravely watching her.

No fool, this Maxie Tarnover. Waremont had been trying to catch his friend's eye. He had been hoping against hope that the servant would not address him as Sir Leigh. Thankfully, this had not happened and other than Kinnaid forgetting himself and playing host, they were momentarily safe. Waremont bent and softly spoke into Maxine's delicate ear. "We have been friends forever. He treats my home and my servants as his own."

"I see," she answered him doubtfully.

Chapter Ten

It was late afternoon. Clouds were moving in, and the sun no longer held center stage. Maxie finished the last of the tasks her aunt had set her and grabbed at her new dark blue cloak as she made for the backstairs and outdoors. What she needed was to walk, to think and be alone to sort out her conflicting sensations.

The visit to Sir Leigh's estate today had left her in a flurry of emotions. Feelings, all of them strong, collided into one another. She needed time to herself. She needed to sort out the jumble in her head. What was this man, this blue-eyed rake of a man? Had he been flirting with her feelings? Faith, yes. No doubt he was bored in the country and needed to dally with a simple country girl in order to pass the time away. She frowned over the notion, not entirely convinced by her own conclusion. There was more that was disturbing about Sir Leigh and Lord Waremont; some mystery that tickled at her brain. Maxie was often guided by her own instincts, and her instincts told her to be wary. Right then, but, why?

She loved her cousin Freddy, but when she suddenly heard his voice at her back, calling her name, she could have screamed. This was not the time for Freddy's absurdities. She needed to think. However, there was nothing for it. She calmed herself and smiled an affectionate greeting. "Hallo, Freddy, just back from town, are you?"

"Yes, and I've got news, Max, wait till I tell you!" Freddy exclaimed portentously.

"Indeed?" laughed Max. "Pray then, do tell me what that may be?"

"Max, it is no laughing matter. Zounds, but you will never credit it. I still find it hard to believe," said Freddy in a tone that held horror.

Max was quick to sense this was no ordinary piece of news and grew serious all at once. "What then, Freddy-boy? What has happened?"

"Murder!" said Freddy in a high pitched voice that was an indication of his distress.

"Murder? What can you mean? Who was murdered? Where?" Max was shocked.

"On Winchelsea Sands. A young girl was found, and Max, Max, we know her!" He shrugged. "At least we have seen her often enough."

Maxine grabbed his arm. "Who, Freddy? Stop giving me bits and pieces. Who was murdered?"

"Anne Bagner. The girl who worked at the fish market for her father, Tom, Toby's good friend. We often saw her with her father and Toby." He shook his head. "Max, they think someone choked her to death with a cord."

"How did she get to Winchelsea Sands? Freddy, that

is quite a distance from Rye." Maxine couldn't believe this. Things like this just didn't happen in their quiet little Romney.

"I don't know. I only know this much because I was standing nearby when the magistrate came to fetch Tom ... to, er ... look ... to identify the body." Freddy shuffled his feet.

"I don't understand. Are they sure she was murdered? Couldn't poor little Anne have drowned?" The sound of her words made her gasp. "Oh, faith ... this is so hideous."

"No, Max. She didn't drown. The magistrate said she was strangled with a cord of some sort."

"Freddy, this is awful. What else do you know?"

Freddy shrugged. "Nought. Toby went with Tom Bagner and I came straight here."

Diverted momentarily, Maxie eyed her cousin. "You were with Toby again?"

"You are not my keeper, Max," Freddy answered her sharply.

"I see," said Maxine quietly. "No, I am not."

Freddy grimaced and then grinned. "Dash it, Max, you aren't my keeper, but, you are my friend. Friends don't go on about things forever. You told me how you felt. I've taken your opinion under consideration. Isn't that enough?"

"I tell you what, Freddy, my buck. We are more than friends. I am your cousin. As your cousin, I might feel it necessary to go any length to save you from danger. Even, taking your father into my confidence. Am I understood?"

Freddy could not be expected to accept this threat graciously. He put up his chin and announced. "That is quite beneath you, cousin." So saying, he stalked off.

Maxine sighed. What to do about Freddy? It certainly was a problem and it was a problem that was not getting better with time, but, worse, so much worse.

The exterior of the Mermaid Inn looked as though its builder had borrowed its design from Shakespearean times. Its lovely mellowed walls of yellow were striped with the rich dark oak beams of another age, all charmingly overgrown with English ivy. Soft lights from candlelight fixtures, and various sized lanterns burned a welcome. The welcome, however, was reserved for sailors, fishermen, flaskers, porters, owlers, smugglers all. The Mermaid was for them, and those willing to rub a friendly shoulder with Romney's popular gentlemen.

The exciseman who entered did so with trepidation and great caution. They knew to ask questions was futile. Their questions would certainly not receive truthful answers. Still, now and then, if only to save face, an excise officer would appear, drink down his ale, give the room a threatening look, and breathe a sigh of relief when he left the Mermaid behind.

As it happened, Waremont and Kinnaid decided that the Mermaid was a perfect place to spend a convivial evening. Each was troubled by thoughts they were as yet unwilling to share. They found a corner table, ordered a bumper of ale each and sat back to watch the antics of the happy crew about them. It wasn't long before they heard talk of the Winchelsea murder. Waremont shot his friend a rueful look.

"The devil you say? Murder, here we are in the peaceful country, and we find ourselves plagued by the crimes of the city?" Waremont reached for a passing barmaid and held her fingers as he gave her a flirtatious smile. "Tell me, my dear, what is this about murder?"

"Oh, aye," said the girl putting a hand to her flushed cheek. "A terrible thing, it is! And me, I know . . . knew Annie. Sech a darlin' girl, m'own friend she was." The barmaid shook her head sorrowfully. "I'll miss 'er I will. Why, we were jest making plans fer Saturday's fair—"

"What happened? Who could have wanted to kill your friend?" asked Kinnaid, much shocked by this.

"She was strangled she was . . . dumped overboard . . . thats 'ow they figure she came up on Winchelsea . . . terrible, terrible . . . Annie was jest the slip of a girl. She wasn't a big strapping wench as m'dad tells me I be. Jest a slip of a girl . . ."

Waremont and Kinnaid eyed one another as the barmaid went off, mumbling sadly to herself about murder and mayhem. Waremont pulled at his lower lip before saying thoughtfully, "Thunder and turf, Leigh, we have walked into a curious situation. Very intriguing."

"What do you mean by that?" Kinnaid shook his head. "We haven't walked into anything." He eyed his friend warily. There was never any telling what Waremont had in his head.

"I mean murder, here in sleepy little Rye? Odd, don't you think?"

"Confound it! No, not when you consider"—he lowered his voice—"that we are in the heart of smuggler's haven. I suppose murder is the norm?"

"You are out there, old boy. Flaskers don't go about killing their children. If she was that barmaid's friend, she couldn't have been any older than what . . . sixteen, seventeen?"

"Yes, well, it is none of our affair, is it?" said Kinnaid irritably, "We have problems enough, don't you think?"

"By Jove, yes, Leigh, yes we do. All the more exciting don't you think . . . juggling all our problems?" Waremont grinned dangerously. "But, this, this is important Leigh. You have a murder in your sleepy little marsh. You are the owner of Romney Grange. You should know what is toward in your own hamlet, don't you think?" Without waiting for a reply, Waremont continued to badger his friend. "Here is some innocent, or not so innocent girl killed by a person unknown. Do you mean to allow her murderer to go free?"

"Don't be flippant," reproved Kinnaid, "And it is not in my power to chase down the poor child's murderer. What? I am not the magistrate. I can not conduct an investigation."

"Ah, but, I don't agree. You are a concerned resident, and a resident of some statue I might add. I think we should pay the magistrate a visit in the morning and see what is being done. I think—"

"Seth!" Kinnaid cut him short. "Who shall we go as? Shall I be you, and you be me? I tell you what, my friend, we were almost in the suds this morning!" Kinnaid shook his head. "What now, shall I tell all my servants to address me as Lord Waremont? What in thunder are we to do? I thought we were undone this morning. What would Miss Huntly—what would any of them have thought of us if we had been exposed during their visit to us? Confound it, Seth, this can not continue. I feel like the worst kind of cad keeping up this pretense of ours. I am sick at heart every single time I think we will be discovered. I only wish we were well out of it. I wish we were on our way back to London."

"What a shockingly fusty fellow you have become old boy. However, be easy about this. We have been in tight situations before and managed. We'll do. See if we don't." Waremont winked at his friend. "The trouble is you have an eye for the Huntly chit. In fact, making a cake of yourself over her. Never saw you enact the fool for a woman before?" Waremont appraised him tauntingly. "Leave it alone, Leigh, it won't do."

"I do not have an eye for Miss Huntly, and why would it not do?"

Waremont smiled. "Because dear boy, how can you pursue a gently born woman under an alias?"

"Damn you, Seth . . . damn you."

Chapter Eleven

Waremont tried to clear his mind as he urged his horse into a steady trot. The evening, though enjoyable, had left him with a head reeling from the after-shocks of one bumper of ale too many. The sky was a grey overcast, and the air was muggy. A low mist hung about the tall grass as he managed his spirited prime blood with sure, purposeful direction.

His lordship was frowning and this had nought to do with his heavy head. Last evening he had teased Kinnaid about his prudish ethics over the fix they were in with the Huntly family. However, the sorry truth was that he, too, was feeling the burden of guilt. The more they saw of the Huntlys, the deeper they were forced to dig their ugly hole. When they had embarked on this lark, he had thought there would be a one meeting, no complications, no strings. Well, he had certainly made a colossal blunder this time! What could he do? Well, he certainly should not be directing his horse toward Huntly Grange? Yet, he could not stop himself as he

headed for the River Rother and the dock. This was
mad. Why was he doing this?

Why, indeed! He knew why. It was the Tarnover chit.

Maxine had mentioned during their conversation yesterday morning, that she often rode out to their dock to
visit the young swan. She had said in that impish style
of hers, that she did so at an early hour so that she
could be comfortable in her breeches.

Waremont grimaced. He knew what he was doing.
There was no question as to what he was doing. He was
riding out at this unholy hour in the sole hope of
meeting a minx of a girl. Damnation. Why? Because she
was an amusing woman, not quite like the women he
had known. She had a refreshing innate honesty he had
never before encountered in the females he had pursued. There too, she stirred his blood, drove his imagination wild. Deuce take it, he was entitled to some
innocent diversion on this bleak morning? Wasn't he?
He would do her no harm. It wasn't his style to seduce
virgins, maids unworthy of the game. No, no. He simply
needed to occupy his time for he dashed well couldn't
sleep. That was all there was to it!

Maxine was clothed in her breeches and short buckskin riding coat as was her habit for her early morning
ride. She had stopped by the dock and found Cyg happily relaxing in the morning mist. She threw him a collection of breads and biscuits, watched him eat, and
then remounted her chestnut gelding. She was restless.
She had not slept well and was preoccupied with her

thoughts. She had not ridden very far when she saw him and felt her blood start to rush to her cheeks. Here he was. He was riding toward her. She could not help but notice how very broad his shoulders were, how expertly he guided his big bay gelding through the tall grass. How his smile made her tremble. And, how very handsome—stop! What was she doing? What could she be thinking? She must not think of him in such terms. He was amusing himself with her while he was in the country. She would not play the fool for someone like that. He was the sort of fellow who would leave on the morrow and never think of her again.

Even with this warning in her head, she could not help, but, offer him a warm welcome as she slowed her horse and awaited his approach, "Good morning to you, Sir Leigh. I must say that you have certainly surprised me. I would not have guessed you to be an early riser."

"And a very good morning to you, Miss Tarnover. It must be an object with me to strive to surprise you whenever possible and thus, perhaps, fix your interest," he said on a low seductive note.

She laughed. "You are bold, sir ... very bold." As blandly as she could manage she asked, "What *does* bring you out here so early?"

He smiled warmly. "You, love. I came in search of you. And Cyg. I must confess an interest in the poor fellow's progress."

Indeed, she told herself at once, attempting to be fair. After all, he had been instrumental in saving Cyg. In fact, he had been the hero of the moment and had never claimed credit. Surely then he was being sincere in his desire to see how Cyg went on after his ordeal? As to fixing his interest with her? She knew better. The art of dalliance was something he had perfected into a sport. He was only having his fun, Max cautioned her heart. Still, she gave him a pretty smile. "Cyg seems to be doing very well thanks to your quick and clever action."

"That young swan has you, only you, to thank for his life. Had you not drawn me into it, I would not even have known he was in trouble."

Maxie blushed. "You *were* wonderful. Don't take that away from yourself," she returned sincerely and her violet eyes met his blue.

"I shan't, especially if it endears me to you," he said softly, and now his eyes found her cherry-hued mouth.

Maxie felt as though somehow her lips had been stroked. She felt her blood rush wildly through her body. This was insane. She would not allow it! Her violet eyes flashed at him. "I certainly did not say that. So, tread easy, Sir Leigh."

He answered her softly, "Still, I should like to endear myself to you, Maxine Tarnover."

They were interrupted at that moment by another early morning rider. Maxie turned to the sound of a horse's snorting and happily exclaimed, "Oh, look . . . it is John, Doctor Wiltshire. I don't suppose you two have met yet? You will like him immensely. Everyone does." She was standing up in her stirrups waving a welcome as the good doctor rode his cob directly up to them.

Sir Leigh inclined his head and softly whispered,

"Later little love . . . I must be off." So saying, he spurred his horse into a canter.

Maxine watched him in some stupefaction, and sure confusion. What was this? One minute he was all concern and gentle caring for a young swan, or so he claimed, and then the next minute he was a callous, arrogant, puffed up in his own consequence fellow! He was being as rude as he had been to her that day in town. It was not at all something she could readily understand. She only hoped that Doctor John did not take it personally.

The good doctor scarcely seemed to notice as he rode up to Maxine and enveloped her with a warm smile. "Hello, Maxine. Still caring for that swan of yours, I suppose?"

"Yes, and he is doing fine, thank you." Maxie beamed at him, "Up and about early. Was it Mrs. Higgins?"

"Aye, her little baby girl decided it was time to enter the world, oh, just about one hour ago." He grinned. "Thought since I was up and about, I might find you here looking in on that young swan of yours." He paused for a moment. "I suppose that was one of the gentlemen from Romney Grange who just left you."

"Yes. He was in a hurry to get back to the Grange." Maxie made light of it.

Doctor John did not seem really interested. He was intent on her and smiled warmly as he said, "Maxine, there is something—"

She cut him off excitedly. "Oh? Have you heard from my publisher?" She frowned, "Oh dear, I hope they aren't going to ask for my next set of stories any earlier than we agreed."

Ruefully John shook his head. "No, Max, that isn't it. Though my man did arrange for vouchers to be directed to a solicitor in London, just as we had agreed. He will receive funds on your behalf in the strictest of confidence and deposit all those funds into your account." He breathed a sigh of relief. "From now on Maxie, you will post all your works to him and he will forward them to your publisher."

"Oh dear. You sound so pleased to be well out of it. I am so very sorry. Have I been a bother? Do forgive me, I had no one else to turn to?" Max was looking distressed.

He reached for her gloved fingers. "No, no, my dear. You misread me . . . completely. I wanted your business conducted in this manner, to leave us free to, well . . ." He shook his head then eyed her quizzically and said, "You know, it is no great scandel for a woman to contribute work to the literary world."

"Still and all, I don't think my aunt would be very pleased, so for the time being, I think I shall strive for anonymity."

"For a young woman who dares the countryside in buckskins and breeches, I find that a very tame attitude." The doctor laughed.

"Have you heard anything new about poor Anne Bagner's murder?"

The doctor stiffened. This was not the sort of thing young women should know of or discuss. He found it supremely annoying. He was, he felt very much enamored with Max. He was thinking of making her his wife. Originally, he had thought to marry Claire, for of the two, Claire had the larger dowry. Now, however, with Maxine's earnings as an author, he thought he would indulge his passion. However, he had very definite notions regarding a female's conduct. "How in blazes did you know about that?"

"Well, Freddy told me. But, by now it is all over town. Something like that can't be, and shouldn't be kept a secret you know."

"I am surprised at Freddy. You are so much in one another's company, that he forgets himself. A gently bred female should not be disturbed with such ugly business."

"I don't agree. Men are forever trying to shield us from what they decide is ugly—"

"Don't you think murder is an ugly business?" he countered.

"I shall not engage in semantics with you, Doctor John." She turned a shoulder on him clearly much insulted.

He laughed. "Truce . . . let us call a truce. It is too late to shield you. What would you have me add to what you already know?"

"Do they have any clue as to who would have done such a thing? Did she really die of strangulation?"

"I don't know whether they have any clues. I don't think so. Yes, she died of strangulation. I was not the examining doctor. Doctor Wrenfield in Winchelsea examined her before it was learned that the poor girl was from Rye."

"This murder just doesn't make sense. Who could possibly want such a young woman dead?" She shook her head of uncovered black glistening tresses. "Do you know that Freddy and I knew her?"

Doctor John frowned at her before asking irritably, "How is that possible? What could you and Freddy have to do with some girl from the fish market?"

"Doctor John, I am surprised at you!" said Max. "At any rate, we only knew her to pass an occasional greeting."

"It is a nasty business, and we should be hopeful that our local magistrate will conduct a thorough investigation."

"Freddy says Mr. Beadle is a fool. He says he doesn't know the first thing about conducting a murder investigation," scoffed Maxine who agreed with her volatile cousin on this point.

"Let us hope that Freddy is wrong about that. After all, how can Freddy know what Mr. Beadle's capabilities are?"

"As to that, I am afraid he is only repeating what he had been told by . . . er . . . town people."

"And that, my dear, is another thing," said Doctor John in what Maxine always felt was his preachers tone. "Frederick spends far too much time with . . . shall we call them, townspeople."

"As to that, no harm will come to Freddy from his town friends."

"Maxine, I am surprised at you. How can you say so? You and I both think that Frederick should be at University, not running amok here in Rye."

"That is a matter best decided by Freddy and his parents."

The doctor did not notice the distance Maxine had put between them. He did not see her chin go up. He did not feel the cold blast of air that frosted her speech. He had no understanding of the ethics that prohibited her from discussing her dear cousin with anyone. The doctor put her answers down as a female's disinterest. A mere woman's uneducated senses to the dangerous lures lurking in Rye for a young man. "Dear Maxine," he said in a most patronizing tone, "his parents, as you well know, dote on young Frederick. They would not say him nay."

"You may be right, but, yea or nay, my dear sir, must come from them." She urged her horse forward, "Now, as much as I always love to chat with you, if I don't get home, bathe and change before my aunt catches me, it will be bellows to mend."

"As much as it goes against the stern proprieties which I dearly uphold, I must admit that I love the sight of you in your britches!"

Maxie inclined her head and called a thank you over her shoulder as she cantered off towards Huntly. He watched her for a long moment. This one must be his. She excited him. He could feel his pulse beating wantonly. Indeed, he had held himself in check far too long!

Chapter Twelve

Maxie couldn't sleep. The day had been full with events that kept bumping into one another in her brain and demanding attention. She finally threw the covers off and scooted into her soft slippers to pad across her cozy room to the latticed window overlooking the gardens. The sky had cleared and there was a full bright moon shining. She smiled to herself for it was so very lovely. She opened the window and felt the night's fresh air stroke her smooth cheeks.

A movement, together with a sound, caught her attention and she turned in its general direction. Peering through the darkness, she found in the moon's full light a very familiar figure. Freddy! Deuce take it, Frederick! What is wrong with you? He was coming away from the River Rother. Were you meeting the owlers? Were you meeting the flaskers? Helping the porters overland?

Max fetched her dressing gown, secured it at her trim waist and quietly went down the corridor to her cousin's room. There she let herself in, took up a chair and waited in the dark.

Six, maybe seven minutes went by and Freddy's door creaked slowly open. Freddy slinked within its portal and nearly jumped out of his skin as Maxine said, "It is three in the morning and I tell you what Frederick Huntly, I will have the truth and I will have it this very minute!"

Freddy's hand had gone to his heart as he gasped in sheer terror. He immediately realized the voice was not emanating from a specter, but, from his cousin and he objected in a strenuous whisper. "Max! You nearly put me under! What the devil are you doing here?"

"No, what the devil are you doing, Freddy? Rum-running?" Max was furious.

"It isn't what you think—" Frederick started to say.

"Don't lie to me, my buck. I saw you. I know what you are at." Max knew how to play the game.

"You saw me?" he was stunned.

"Why, Freddy? You will end in ruining your family's name. Is that what you want?"

"No, no. I went to the river to warn them that the porters wouldn't be there with the wool—they had heard there was a trap laid. It was my job to warn Tob—to warn the owlers, that's all."

"Your job? Since when was a Huntly ever hired for such work?" Maxine could have slapped his face. This went beyond larking. This went beyond high spirits.

Freddy hung his head. "I was in no danger of being caught."

"Were you not? *I* caught you. I am just a slip of a

woman and I caught you, Frederick! Of all the mad, harebrained fetchs you have ever ..." She started for the door, she simply could not continue to speak when she was this angry. She did not want to say anything that she would regret. It wasn't wise to handle a situation that needed good sense and reason, when her temper was out of control.

"What are you going to do?" he asked in a small boy's voice.

"Indeed. Tell me, Frederick Huntly, what are you going to do, and you just might have my answer. We *will* speak in the morning. And, Freddy, you will do more listening than you have these six months and more. Depend upon it!" So stating, Maxine stormed from the room.

Freddy moved to drop onto his bed in some consternation. He was in for it now. He adored Maxine. She was cousin, she was friend. He could not help but admire his Max. Just look at her now. She would not, could not be hoodwinked. His parents? Of course he loved them, but, they hadn't a clue about what made him tick. They adored him, but they adored the picture they had of him. Max always cared enough to be there ... to know, to feel for him. Max had always understood. Even now, as angry as she was, she knew and she understood. That she would not tolerate his wayward behavior was even in this bleak hour, a thing that he respected in her. He loved Max and it saddened him that she was presently so very, very disappointed in him.

Damn, but he was not looking forward to the morning. He was in for a rare trimming, that was certain.

Zounds! He was ill just thinking about it. He pulled off his muddied boots and dropped them with a thud. He felt wretched. He was a shocking fellow. Very sadly he owned himself a gapeseed for he had certainly made a mull of it.

Feeling badly hipped he dropped his remaining clothing in a heap on the carpet covering his nicely polished wood floor. Sighing heavily he climbed into his large four poster bed. How was he ever going to sleep with this now hanging over his withered future, he asked himself silently as he laid his head on his soft pillow and promptly began snoring.

Morning found Maxie up bright and early, but instead of her usual riding outfit of buckskin and breeches, she was clothed in a morning gown of soft pink muslin. Her black hair she had arranged neatly at the top of her head. She was pacing in her room, thinking out what she would say to Freddy. It was an extremely delicate situation because she simply could not threaten something she wasn't going to do. Betray Freddy to his father? Absolutely not. That would be a backhanded thing to do. It would not serve. Right then, Maxie, how do you control him?

A scratch sounded at her door and with a brow up she went and pulled it open with some determination. There, she was surprised to find Claire, not only up and about at an unusual hour for her, but dressed very prettily in a riding outfit of dark green velvet.

"Claire? Well, and good morning. Never say you are actually going riding *now?*"

She blushed. "Well, no, not quite yet, but I wanted to try on this habit and see what you think?" She twirled round as she spoke.

"Perfect. It suits you. Now, what is this all about?"

As an answer, Claire shoved a piece of ivory note-paper into Max's hand, "Read this."

Max did as she was told and came up smiling wickedly, "Well, well, well. It is precisely as I told you yesterday. I said, Claire, that rake Waremont has a tendré in your direction. Oh, but, no, you said giggling all the while." Maxie waved the notepaper. "Ha!"

Claire turned several shades of red and clasped Maxie's hand. "Do not say so, Maxine. Besides, he extends the invitation to you as well."

"Because he is no fool! What, should he invite you to ride the Grange and then picnic *alone* with him? I don't think so. He needs me for propriety."

"Do you mind? Will you find it terribly boring?" Claire asked anxiously.

"Absurd girl. I shall find it too terribly amusing ... watching you and Waremont make sheep eyes at each other. Faith, but, this is good. Famous Waremont, marauder of hearts, struck down by my dear, sweet Claire! Excellent." She linked her arm through her cousin's and said brightly, "Come then, we shall breakfast together so that I can tease you unmercifully."

They were laughing together as they met Peltons in the breakfast parlor. Claire stopped to ask after her parents. Peltons inclined his head and answered regally as

was his style. "Your father, Miss Claire, has gone off
with his bailiff for the day. Your mother is taking her
breakfast in her room as she has the headache."

"And Freddy?" requested Maxie now suspicious.

"Mr. Frederick did inquire after you, Miss Maxine,
and upon learning that you were not yet out of your
room, he said he was going out to join his father and the
bailiff."

Maxine could have stamped her foot. Why the little
devil, she thought as she groomed her temper into silence. Well, well. Never mind Max. He can put off, but,
not escape the inevitable. Suddenly, a notion came to
mind, and as she followed Claire to the buffet table the
idea took on strength. By the time she was seated and
buttering her toast, she knew exactly what she was going
to do!

Chapter Thirteen

Waremont's blue eyes appraised Kinnaid's face over the breakfast table. "Blister it, never say you did? I don't believe it. I think you have gone mad, Leigh." He put down his coffee cup, to continue to give his best friend his scathing opinions. "Have maggots attacked your brain? What is wrong with you? You are making a cake of yourself!"

"I don't see what all the fuss is about?" objected Kinnaid avoiding his friend's eyes.

"Oh, don't you, my hale man? Don't you? Give it up, Leigh, it just won't fadge."

"I don't see that. Want to . . . want the pleasure of Miss Huntly's company on a ride around the Grange . . . picnic afterwards. No one about, no servants to call my name in question . . . it serves, Seth. What could go wrong?"

"I think it puts you, and me by association, even deeper into the hole we would like to be well out of, my buck!" snapped Waremont, very much on edge this morning. "What could you have been thinking? And did you expect Miss Huntly to accompany you unchaperoned?"

"Don't be absurd. Of course not. I invited Miss Tarnover to join us."

"You did what?" Waremont's temper exploded as he ran his hands through his hair. This was worse than all the rest.

"Look Leigh, I got us into this havey-cavey mess and I am most certainly honor bound to get us out of it, as cleanly as I may. Pulling a stunt like this, after we had decided not to call upon the Huntlys again is not comprehensible. It makes things far more difficult."

A servant appeared at that moment with a silver salver. This he presented to Sir Leigh, who glanced guiltily first at Waremont before he took up the sealed notepaper. Still not looking at his waiting friend he quickly read the note. Attempting to repress the joy he felt, he said, not quite without feeling, "They have accepted my invitation and mean to meet me by the dock at noon."

"Splendid, my boy!" Waremont's acrimonious tone was nearly as deadly as the look he cast Kinnaid.

Having discarded her pretty morning gown for her new riding ensemble of royal blue, Maxine was making the short trip into town, and down to the quay. She had promised Claire that she would return in plenty of time to accompany her on their excursion to meet with Lord Waremont. They were, this Lord Waremont and her cousin Claire, amazingly suited for one another. Both glowed when they looked at each other. But what Max could not match was the picture Lady Waremont had drawn of her son with the actual man. It was a puzzle that nagged at her intuitive brain. It was most odd. However, at the moment she had another very real problem to attend.

Fishing vessels were just returning with their day's catch. It was a busy morning on the docks. Maxie went to a nearby livery and had her horse taken to a stall to await her return. She knew just where she was going and it was with some determination that she wielded her way through the crowd of shoppers, hawkers, sailing crews, and idle tourists to Toby's boat. The Sweet May it was called in his mother's memory. It had been one of the things she had liked about Toby. He hadn't a wife or children, but, he had a profound respect for family. She had enjoyed the little sailing trips he had taken her and Freddy on the summer before. She had loved hearing his wild stories of the sea. She saw him now at his stern, mending a sail and she could not help but give him a warm smile, "Captain Toby?" she called, "How are you?"

"Well, lass . . . very well, Now, it has been many a day since ye've come to pay old Toby a visit." He moved to help her on board. "Aye then, lass, I can see ye 'ave a bone to pick wit me. So, then, best get on wit it. Speak yer mind. I'm not one fer mincing me words, and I don't think ye be sech as that either!"

"Direct speaking suits me just fine, Captain Toby, so I'll tell you to your face straight out, that I did not think to see you ill use my cousin, Frederick."

"Did I do that, lass?" There was sadness in his faded eyes.

"It is beginning to look that way to me, though, in truth, I do find it so very hard to believe."

"And, Freddy-boy told ye then that I misused him in some way? He told ye that, did he?'

"No, of course not. Freddy thinks you are the sun, the stars, and the moon. I wish he did not, but, he does," she said on a sigh.

"Frederick is a good lad." He shook his head. "He'll do."

"Toby, don't you see. He shouldn't be aping your style of life. He shouldn't be sneaking off in the dead of night to ... to what? Be a watchdog for the owlers?"

"I did not ask the lad for that. I been trying to keep 'im at a distance. I want no 'arm to come to 'im and ye should know that."

"Then what was he doing down at our dock last night? Toby, what were you doing down there? Your antics might involve the Huntly name. I can not stand by and allow that."

"Can't ye now? Whot then, miss?"

"Toby, don't you see. Won't you stop? What you are doing is wrong."

"*Wrong?* Laws are made by men who know nothing about how sech as I 'ave to live. Don't be telling me whot is wrong."

"Yes, Toby, I understand, at least sometimes I do." she shook her head, "Still—"

"Ye be talking on things ye know nuthin' about," Toby shot back angrily. "Ye talk loike we be cut-throats and sech." He shook his head sadly. "I thought ye knew better."

"I do know better. I swear it. I know that you think you are simply trying to make a living—"

"I be doing more than making a living, as ye call it missy!" Toby shot back. "Lord bless ye, I be making a cry to the Crown! Don't ye know? The sheep farmers, they be forced to sell their wool to the mill owners 'ere at 'ome at prices our government says is fair; but the farmer, he be starving and the mill owner, he be getting rich. What think you is fair? Eh? So, they be other markets whot needs our English wool. Those markets pay a fair price. Aye, missy, you tell me then, what's right, what's wrong?" He shook his head and the anger was still there in his face. "Whot can we do? Who would listen to us? We manage in our own way, by our own rules. We owlers, we do our job and there be no one getting 'urt." He looked away from her as he scanned the sea. "Aye then, we owlers send off the wool to them overseas whot pays a fair price. It don't suit ye, but, ye don't worry about keeping a roof over yer pretty 'ead. Aye then, a nice fine 'ot dinner always awaits ye. No lass, don't be preaching to me, about things beyond yer ken. It won't serve."

Maxine felt a sure sense of shame rinse over her body. Was she so wrong? Of course she was wrong. She had passed judgement on them without consideration to the entire picture. Her father used to always say that things were never just black and white, but full of shades, so many shades. However, Freddy was not one of these men. He was a Huntly on a lark. He was not motivated by the same concerns. He had no right to run with the owlers. She inclined her head. "I am so very sorry. I had not considered your situation. However, Freddy owes it to do what he can for you *only* from a legal standpoint. One day he will be able to fight for causes such as yours, but only if he is a viable, credible citizen. What he is doing now, neglecting his education, running amok with you, will not serve his future and it could end in hurting him and his entire family."

"Now lass, we be on the same ground. Aye then, I been telling the boy to go back to school. I been telling 'im I don't want to be finding 'im at m'elbow every toime I turn around. Do he listen? No, 'ee do not! I didn't ask 'im fer the warning last evening, but, 'ee got wind of it and come on 'is own to warn us. Tis a good lad 'ee is, and methinks, ye yerself might 'ave done the same."

"Now what makes you think that, sir?" Maxie peeped up at him.

"Lord love ye, girl, I knows whot I knows. Ye been looking out fer the lad. Ye discovered whot 'ee was about last night. Ye took 'im in hand yerself I'd wager, but, ye didn't blab, did ye? No, ye didn't go running to his father, but came 'ere to me to talk it out straight. Ye would 'ave done the same as Freddy did fer an old friend . . . and I always counted meself one of yers."

"You are quite right, Captain Toby, you are a friend. Perhaps between us we can make Freddy go up to University." She sighed.

"I 'ave me 'opes, I do. Tis time and now ye got the means, don't ye, lass?"

* * *

Doctor John had finished his business on the quay and started towards the livery where he had left his horse and gig. A passing hawker, a lovely girl selling fresh baked tarts, caught his eye and his attention as he realized he was hungry. He stopped to purchase a pastry, and was exchanging pleasantries with the woman, when another girl on a vessel not so very far away, caught his eye. Maxine? What the devil was she doing with that man? Without another word he started off towards the Sweet May.

"Maxine!" Doctor John called in shocked accents.

Maxie turned to the sound of her name. She was taken aback at the sharpness of Doctor John's tone.

"Well, and good morning, Doctor John," she called sweetly. "What brings you here so early?"

"I might ask you the same question," he answered indicating by his expression that he certainly did not approve of her being there.

Maxie had long ago learned to look after herself. Her aunt had been pleased enough with the arrangement, though now and then she would complain to her husband about Maxine's independent nature.

Max knew of course that it might look odd for her to be on the Sweet May, alone with Captain Toby. However, she would not be scolded by Doctor John. It was not his place to monitor her activities.

"I?" she answered, her hackles well up, her violet eyes warning and her delicate brow arched. "Why, I am visiting a friend, a very dear friend." She then touched

Captain Toby's forearm and apologized, "Do forgive me, but, I must rush off. Claire needs me, and I must not be even one moment late, or I shall find my cousin ready to offer me violence." She waved herself off, leaving Toby looking thoughtfully after her.

She turned and found Doctor John's hand extended, ready to assist her. Gracefully, she allowed him to lend her his hand and then his arm as she disembarked, and walked beside him in rigid silence for a long moment.

Doctor John was no fool. He could see that he had offended her. He attempted to make light of it and offered her a smile. "Contrary to your expectations, I shall not scold."

She eyed him and then relented with one of her ready smiles. "I am glad."

"Yes, but, all the same, I feel compelled to ask you just what you were doing with *that* man?"

"I, however, do not feel compelled to answer," returned Max sweetly.

"I was under the impression that we are good friends," he said on a grave note.

She turned to him at once. He had helped her so very much with her work, how could she turn him up cold? This was Doctor John. He was so very dear to her, she chastised herself. She touched his arm and looked up at him. "You know very well that we are friends. You have displayed yourself a true friend and have helped me in a very private matter. As your friend, you may expect me to rush to your aid. You may expect me to stand by you in hard times and take your part. You may expect to enjoy my company and allow me to enjoy yours. However, as my friend, you may not govern me."

He was lost a moment in the beauty of her violet eyes. His gaze shifted to her lips. He wanted her. He could almost taste her. He smiled softly to say, "As you wish. I shall contrive to restrict my over-protective behavior in your regard. I can see you want none of it!"

She thought it wise to leave it at that. "How good you are, Doctor John."

"If I overstepped, it was, well, Maxine, you must know how much I care?"

They had nearly reached the stables. All at once, Maxine realized that her good friend was intimating at feelings that went beyond mere friendship. She was immediately flattered. She blushed and she lowered her eyes. However, she knew at once that she did not feel the same. His eyes seemed to burn through her and she knew a need to escape him. How dreadful. This was Doctor John. He was an adored friend. What had happened? They had reached the stables and as she saw the stableboy coming toward her, took the opportunity to motion to him for her horse.

She returned her attention to the doctor, and gave him an apologetic smile. "I must go."

He took her gloved hand and held it tightly, "I shall contrive to see you on the morrow. Perhaps you would like to take a ride with me to Hastings?"

"I should dearly love a visit to Hastings, but I am afraid my aunt has a few tasks for Claire and me to attend to . . . oh, here is my horse." She turned to receive the reins of her chestnut and found she could not meet

Doctor John's eyes. Fortunately, he offered to give her a
leg up and she was able to divert her attention to ar-
ranging her skirt.

"I do so prefer riding astride. This is such a nuisance.
It is a woman's clothing that prevents her from being all
that she could be." Maxie laughed merrily and waved
over her shoulder as she left the doctor behind.

Lord Waremont's blue eyes followed Maxie's every
move. He watched her depart and then returned his attention to the doctor. It was obvious to him, that the
two had something of a spat and then had very quickly
made it up. He found it all very disconcerting. Why he
should was more than he could fathom, but, there it
was. Well, he had not discovered very much more than
they already knew about the poor girl's murder during
his visit to the local magistrate. He had been on his way
to the livery to retrieve his horse when he had spotted
Maxine.

He had been riveted in place for he could not believe
how very ravishing a creature she was in her stunning
royal blue habit. She stood on board a weathered schoon-
er, conversing easily with its weathered captain as though
it were the most natural thing in the world.

He stood watching her, mesmerized by her flitting expressions. She certainly was unlike all the rest of the
women he had known. What the devil was she doing
with this older sailor? He and Max were obvious friends.

He frowned to himself, for it was also obvious that
Max and the local doctor were friends . . . very good

friends! Well, he hadn't planned on joining Kinnaid's little picnic, but, now, he rather thought he might! He continued his walk towards the livery.

Chapter Fourteen

"Claire, stop fussing. You look beautiful. That shade of green is very flattering," Maxie addressed her cousin banteringly as they rode their horses toward the River Rother and the dock. Maxie could see Claire still seemed uncertain and giggled as she shook her head. "Believe me, Claire, you look entrancing."

"Really? But my hair? Are my ringlets becoming a mess? It is so windy and my hat doesn't feel right. Is it sitting in place?"

"Your hat is sitting very properly on your fine head, and your ringlets are ringlets still. I am most assuredly persuaded that even if your hair were a mass of knots, your new beau would like the look of you all the same. It is my belief that when one falls in love, one looks past the façade of a person and finds the soul. It is the soul you fall in love with, the soul that creates the truth of your smile on your lips, in your eyes . . ."

"Maxie, stop. He is not in love with me. He doesn't

know who I really am. He can't see to my soul. Why, we hardly know each other," Claire objected.

"Oh, is that so? Then why are you so very anxious to see him again? Why are you quaking and trembling from head to foot? I have never seen you behave this way for any man ever before."

There was no time for more as the gentleman in question had just ridden over the crest of the hill and was now trotting his gelding towards them. The smile in his grey eyes and on his thin lips was warm as he looked to Claire.

"Hallo!" he called as he approached and included Maxie in his welcoming smile. "Haven't we a lovely day for our outing?"

"Oh, yes . . ." Claire's voice was nearly breathless.

Maxine almost grinned like a pixie, so great was her amusement as she watched these two. "Where, my lord, did you put our luncheon? I do not see it on your person or on your horse. I must tell you that I am starving nearly to death!"

"Well now, I certainly can not allow a lady in my company to starve to death. What would people think?" He laughed. "Never fear, my people are at this very moment taking a wagonload of delicious food to a very pretty spot for our picnic. I thought, first, we might enjoy a short ride along the river?"

"Oh! How very clever of you, my lord," exclaimed Claire who then blushed a dark shade of pink.

"Room for one more?" called a familiar male voice at their backs.

Maxine was conscious of her heart. Suddenly it was

beating at a dangerous rate. What the deuce was wrong with her? It was *only* that blue eyed devil, Sir Leigh. Nothing to panic about, and yet, she felt her blood tingling her body as he rode closer to them and his smile enveloped her.

Sir Leigh was heartily welcomed by his friend, for now.

The baronet urged his horse to fall in step beside Maxine's gelding. He smiled and said softly. "I noticed you on the docks this morning, and would have tried to win your attention, but, alas, you were so engrossed, too engrossed to notice me."

She looked at him sideways and considered the tone of his words. He spoke gently, without apparent guile, but Maxie was not so green as that. She recognized at once what he was at and said lightly, "Indeed, I had such a busy morning."

"I love the smell of the salt water. I have yet to talk Le—Seth."—he quickly corrected "—into a walk along the beach." He smiled warmly at her. "Though Rye Harbor with the fishing fleet is quite a beautiful sight. I like the design of your friend's boat Sweet something?"

Maxie was not taken in by his backroad tactic. She was however, willing to play his game. "Oh yes, Toby's Sweet May. Freddy and I have often enjoyed summer sailing with him, though I haven't gone off with them in some months."

"No doubt, Freddy still sails with Toby."

Maxie hestiated only a fraction of a moment and her eyelashes flickered. "Yes, Freddy loves the sea." She smiled idly.

"So, there I was, finishing up my business with your local magistrate and hoping to catch you up when you left your sailor, but there was your doctor taking over, the very one you wanted to introduce me to yesterday. I would have spoken to you then, but you seemed to be having a very serious discussion and I did not wish to intrude."

"Nonsense! I am certain Doctor John would have been happy to finally meet you." Maxie's innate honesty forced her to say, and with a sideways glance, *"I* would have been happy for the interruption!"

Waremont laughed. "Really? I had the distinct impression that you thought the world of this wondrous Doctor John?"

"Oh, I do, but, I dislike being, shall we say, managed, even when one thinks it's for my own good. Doctor John is very dear friend, but he thinks I must be shielded from things that are in the realm of what *I* consider my own business."

"And you have not given him the right to do that, yet?"

Slowly, she responded. "I, have given no one that right . . . and I am not certain I ever shall." She eyed him consideringly, "Now, it is my turn to ask a question or two? Don't you think?"

He laughed. "You may always ask, if you do not always expect an answer."

"It is a simple thing and since you mentioned the matter, I take it, that tis not off limits," she smiled charmingly at him.

"Now what could you be talking about? What simple

thing is it that you want to know, my little love?" His
blue eyes were alive with dancing lights as he watched
her flitting expressions. She was an enchanting creature,
full of naughtiness, willfulness, yet, absolutely breath-
taking. But, it was more than mere beauty that captivated and mesmerized him to stare at her in wonder. It
was the way her violet eyes had of laughing, and the
way she had of crinkling up her pert nose. It was
the way she would arch a look at him. It was something
deep inside of her that glowed in her face, in her aura.
Damnation! but, she was a fine, fine woman. He loved
the softness of her smile, the music of her giggle, the the
. . . stop! Since when was he taken-in by such wiles?
This was preposterous. "Well, then, sweet love, ask
away?" he urged, trying to put a halt to his wayward
thoughts.

Maxie's violet eyes were alive with mischief. "I am
not your love, sweet, or otherwise. What I want to know
is why did you visit our local magistrate. If it is about
private matters, then of course you should tell me to
mind my manners, but, if it is about poor Annie's murder, I should very much like to know if he had anything
further to report?"

Blister it! What had induced him to mention his visit
to the magistrate this morning? He had of course gone
as himself, not wishing to carry the lie of his identity all
over town. If Maxie were to speak to the fellow, he
would say that Waremont, not Sir Leigh had visited
him. Well, there was nothing for it, but to brazen it out.
Perhaps she would not even have any occasion to speak
to the dratted fellow.

"You wound me to the quick. I protest, you are most certainly my love, and though I realize what you are trying to tell me is that I am not *your* love, this is what I mean to endeavor to be." He said, putting one hand to his heart.

"I take leave to tell you that your behavior is outrageous and quite wicked, for if I were just a green girl, I might be taken-in by such pretty talk and then suffer a decline when you return to London and forget me," said Maxie, putting the back of her hand to her forehead for a dramatic affect. She then sat up straight and beamed happily. "Now that we are clear on that, do you intend to answer my question?"

His head went back as he released a yelp of laughter. *"Minx.* You do want manners!"

"Ah, then it was not about the murder?" Maxie lowered her eyes, "I am so very sorry—"

"Stop! You know very well it was about the murder, but gently-bred females should not be inquiring about the details of such ugly events."

"Now you sound just like my dear doctor," scoffed Maxine. "It is a backward male point of view."

"You sound like the Godwin sisters." There was a light in his eyes and his glance stroked her affectionately.

"Then I must be proud. I have read and enjoyed some of their essays."

"Then when you come to London, and I am persuaded that you must come to London, I will introduce you to them. I consider them amongst my very dear friends." Lunatic, he told himself at once. How was he ever to introduce her to anyone? He was living a lie.

"I would like that, but you may be sorry you made such a promise for I may hold you to it. There is a very good chance that I shall be visiting London . . . in the near future." She smiled mischievously. "I would not have thought you would approve of such women. They are considered, I understand, quite radical."

"And very interesting. One must ever be ready to discuss and understand points of views other than one's own"—he grinned then—"even if they come from women."

"Then tell me what is happening? What does Mr. Beadle know? Are they getting closer to solving Annie's murder?" She lowered her lashes against her cheek, "Freddy and I used to see her quite often working at her father's fish stall. We knew her well enough to say hallo in passing and I just want to know that Mr. Beadle is working diligently."

He could see that she was in earnest and it was more than idle curiosity. She was a complex being, very different from most of her gender. "I am sorry. I did not realize that you were acquainted with the poor child. I am told she had not even reached her eighteenth birthday."

"Freddy told me that. It is a thing inconceivable to me, that a man, any man, could have tied a cord around her throat and taken her young life away. She was a sweet girl. Who could have done that to her? Does Mr. Beadle have any clues?"

"If he did, he did not tell me. All he would say was that he was working strenuously to find her murderer."

"Well then, it is as Freddy says. Mr. Beadle is a fool. She can't have been taken away, murdered and left in

Winchelsea without someone knowing something. Freddy says that Beadle is too lazy to do a real investigation. He says Tom, Annie's father, means to find the villain and deal with him."

"Would that he could." said Waremont thoughtfully.

"Oh, he will. Tom Bagner is very well liked in Rye. He will put the pieces of the puzzle together and he will have his man."

"Now, is that what Freddy says? Or, is the woman, Miss Tarnover expressing her own opinion?"

"Why sir, a woman is always smart enough to listen to the facts, and then make up her own mind . . . and change it when necessary." Max laughed throatily at this as she urged her horse into a canter.

He was conscious of desire. What was wrong with him? He was behaving like a schoolboy! Still, he grinned at the sound of her laughter and followed suit, ready, so ready to play!

Chapter Fifteen

The day had been wonderful. Maxine could not remember ever feeling the exhilaration she had felt from
the moment Sir Leigh had joined their little party. He
was so different from any other man she had ever known.
He was witty, clever and he had a way of drawing the
best out of her. She must not, could not think of him in
that way. It would only lead to heartache. Her intuition
was working overtime. Something was out of place. She
wasn't quite sure what it was, but, there was a tickle in
her logic that she couldn't quite fix and it was whenever
she was with Waremont and Sir Leigh together.

Today, there had been something odd about Sir
Leigh when he nearly called Lord Waremont by his own
name, Leigh. And Lord Waremont was bothersome. For
no clear reason, she felt, he was not comfortable with
his own title. It was as though he were shy to owning up
to his noble lines. It was most odd. However, she had no
time now for such silliness.

She moved to her window. It was growing late and

would soon be time to descend for dinner. Freddy was still *not* home. He had not returned with his father. Upon her inquiring after him, her uncle had said that Freddy had announced he had some business or other in town but that he would certainly be home in time for dinner. Yes, yes, right and tight, Frederick Huntly! Avoiding me, eh? Maxine thought irritably. Well, she would not be able to have at him during dinner with the entire household present, but he was gravely mistaken if he thought she would not get to him in the end. Indeed, Freddy-boy, she said to herself, it grows much worse for you every minute!

Tom Bagner, with the help of his daughter, had maintained their little cottage just the way his dear wife had left it before she died last year. Now, his little one was gone, too. He bent his head in his hands and sank down onto the kitchen chair his wife had painted so lovingly years ago and let out a stifled cry.

Toby was at the kitchen door, the top half of which was open wide. Beside him was Freddy. He heard his good friend's anguish and felt his heart break for the man. He put a finger to his lips and motioned to Freddy to back up. Having done this he made a clatter of noise before calling out, "Tom! You in there, Tom?"

Tom Bagner quickly wiped the tears from his cheek with the back of his well-worn sleeve. He sniffed himself into control and loudly, gruffly to hide the tremor in his voice called out a welcome. "Aye, Toby. In wit ye!" he said as he jumped up from his chair.

Toby slipped off his hat as he entered the neat little kitchen, put out his hand and touched Tom's shoulder. "Not gonna be asking ye 'ow ye be doing mate, think I know. Came by with Freddy 'ere, 'ee wants to pay 'is respects. There now, seat yerself down, and old Toby will put on the kettle. I've got somethin' to tell ye, but, we best be talking over some nice hot tea and I'll be lacing it with a ball of fire, with yer leave. T'will do us all some good." He moved to make himself busy over the fire. Smiling he added on a light note, hoping to give Tom a distraction, "Ah now, 'ere it is? He held up a bottle of brandy. "This will be young Freddy's first taste of this in his tea I think."

"Whot? Tell me Freddy-boy never 'ad a bit of heart in his tea? That be a rare wheedle ye be cutting, then Toby!" Tom scratched at his whiskers.

"Lord love ye, man, but, tis no whisker." He turned to Freddy who had his chin well up, "Tell 'em lad."

"What? Of course I have had a hot toddy." I'm out of petticoats, you know."

"Hot toddy?" ejaculated Tom momentarily diverted. "Hot toddy? This ain't no hot toddy." He pulled out a chair and motioned for Freddy to sit. Took up his chair once more and watched Toby at the stove. He waited a moment more for Toby to put out the mugs and sit with them at the round dark oak table before asking, "Whot then, 'ave ye got? Is it about m'girl? I be that sick Toby. Sick wit meself for not 'aving more of an eye to 'er comings and goings, but she was ever a good girl . . . never came in late . . . not so that I'd be worried. I shouldn't be 'ere pining. I should be out there looking fer the devil

whot killed 'er, but I jest ain't been able to do nought."
Tom felt the tears well up, he felt his voice falter and
looked away.

"Never ye mind. Ye got friend's don't ye? Aye, then
we'll do. Me, and the lads, we been doing some quiet
nosing around. Not attracting no attention like." He
studied Tom for a long moment before asking, "Did little Annie ever mention having an eye for any one lad?
Did she, well, did she mayhap, tell ye she had any feelings for one lad in particular?"

"Thats jest it! I disremember Annie ever eyeing anyone. At least, not so I would notice. She never did own
to any sech feelings, not to me." He shook his head.
"But, damn my soul! She wouldn't have. She knew I
wouldn't loike it. My girl wasn't even eighteen. I wasn't
ready to give 'er over to jest anybody."

"Well, I got to tell ye, that there was someone." He
put up his hand, "Don't know who it was, but it seems
one day she was talking wit Bess over at the Mermaid,
and Bess says Anne let slip that she thought she was falling in love. When Bessy tried to get more out of her, little Anne jest clammed up and went on her way. That
was only a few days ... before they ... er found yer
girl." Toby closed his eyes a moment. Tom was jumping
to his feet with his hands clenched into fists at his sides.

"Toby, are ye telling me ... it was someone she knew
... someone she trusted?"

"It do look that way, fer if not, why hasn't 'ee come
forward, at least to you, to pay his respects?" Toby
shook his head sadly. "Never fret it, Tom. We mean to
find this cull and if it was 'im whot did this terrible, ter-

rible thing. 'Ee'll pay, depend upon it. We don't mean to let 'im get away wit his piece of knavery." He bade Tom sit again and shoved the mug into his hand. "Trust me in this old friend. 'Ere now, drink up."

Freddy took all this in with wide eyes and unconsciously sipped at his tea, upon which he promptly choked and kept choking until Toby was forced to heartily, laughingly slap at his back. The laughter relieved the tenseness of the moment.

Dinner at Huntly Grange that same evening proved to be an extremely trying experience for poor Mr. Huntly. His daughter, was not herself. She seemed to be in a cloud and he had twice to repeat himself to her in order to be heard. His wife was in high spirits and chatted on about absurdities that nearly drove him out of his mind. Then there was Freddy sunk in his chair, scarcely uttering a word and if he was not mistaken, he had more than once caught his niece glowering threateningly toward his son.

He had long ago learned how to preserve his peace and sanity. As soon as the meal was at an end, he excused himself and hurriedly went off to his study to enjoy his pipe and some light reading. Mrs. Huntly requested her daughter to attend to her upstairs. Claire was extremely deft with needlework and her mother wished her to assist her with one of her patterns. This left Freddy to Maxine's mercy.

Freddy very unwisely attempted a quiet escape, but

Max blocked the doorway and with arms akimbo, inquired, "Going somewhere, Freddy?"

He eyed her stubbornly for a moment and then caved-in.

"No, no . . . we are not playing at ducks and drakes, my love," she said gravely, "We are going to talk. We are going to come to an understanding and we are going to do that, here and now!"

Freddy moved over to an oversized winged chair and plopped down heavily. He didn't speak and he did not look at his cousin. He knew he had this lecture coming, and with noble resolve he had resigned himself to it.

Maxie eyed him consideringly for a long moment before deciding to alter her tactic. She went to move a chair so that she could face him. This done she leaned over and touched his knee. "Freddy? You would be bored to tears if I went on and on about the duty you owe to the people of your town. So I shan't do that. You need an education. You may not want it, but, you understand why you need it." She shrugged her dainty shoulders. "It is clear, don't you think?"

He eyed her gloomily. "So that is it, eh? You mean to make me go up to Cambridge. I suppose I have no choice in the matter? I imagine you mean to tell m'father about last night if I don't agree to your terms. Well, you hold the cards on this, don't you, cousin?" there was a bitterness in the sound of his words.

"No Freddy, I don't mean to make you do anything. It is my belief that you do yourself, your name, your people, a great disservice by foregoing an education. However, if you feel you want to lark away your youth and live like a nodcock, then so be it. I do not admire it, but, it is your choice." She paused for effect.

"As to forcing you to it by telling your father about your indescretion last evening, I am surprised at you. Freddy, I thought you knew me better than that. We have always been friends. If you wish to discuss your activities with your father, it is up to you to do so. I certainly would never dream of doing anything so back-handed."

Freddy went forward and took Maxie's hands to hold them tightly, "You are a great gun, Max. I knew you wouldn't do that—I knew it."

"Of course not, Freddy. However, I want you to be a brave lad and think about doing something, not because you want to, but, because it is the wise thing, the right thing to do."

He looked down at his feet. "Aye, you want me to go up to university? You want me to take up my studies again. I know." He sighed sadly.

"I do, with all my heart. Freddy, you have good friends there ready to welcome you into their fold. I do think you may find it a different and enjoyable experience. It isn't school as you knew it. I think you may expect a great deal of freedom at Cambridge." She looked hopefully at him.

He laughed. "I doubt that." He sighed heavily. "Right then, I shall think about it. Truly, you have my word as a gentleman."

"Thank you," said Max, thinking she had won a major battle.

"Maxie, I have a bit of news to tell you . . . and don't

be scolding me for going into town. It wasn't just to see
Toby, but, to go over and pay our respects to Tom
Bagner, poor chap."

"Oh, yes. You were quite right to do so," said Max
sympathetically, "I mean to drive over to visit with him
tomorrow with a basket of cook's meat pies. I am sure
Tom has not been eating well. I shall take Claire with
me."

"Thank you, Max. You are the best of good girls, for
it is true, he looks like he hasn't been eating. He is sadly
ailing, wants to find his daughter's murderer and we
know Beadle just isn't the man to do it." He looked at
Max for a long moment. "Toby is, though."

"I won't argue that point, Freddy. Toby knows everyone in and around Rye."

"Max, he has already found out something." Freddy
said on a hushed note of excitement.

"What?" Maxie's eyes opened wide.

"Annie had a beau," Freddy said portentiously.

Maxie looked puzzled. "There is nought in that." She
shook her head over it. "Many girls have beaus. She
was, after all, seventeen."

"Toby says it means something. Toby says it doesn't
look good for this man, whoever he is because he hasn't
come forward to own up to his friendship with Anne.
Toby says his insides are twitching over it and that his
insides are never wrong."

"Ah, Toby's insides. Well then, that makes a vast deal
of difference," said Maxie her eyes twinkling.

"Maxine!" He reproached her. "I did not think you
would make light of this. Indeed, I thought of all people,

you would understand such things. You are forever telling me that you *feel* this, that you *sense* that. You have always called it your woman's intuition. Right then, I have always believed you. I've always accepted it. Some times certain things can not be explained. Well, Toby has instincts of his own, and he says his instincts think we should find this mysterious beau of Anne's and I agree."

"You have made an excellent point and I do beg your pardon. Now, I mean to retire to my room, and get some of my scribbling done." Fred was the only other person other than Doctor John who knew about Maxine's success with her writing.

"You know Max, if *we* helped Toby solve this, you could write about it, almost as a tribute to Anne."

"Now, how could you and I help Toby in this?" Max was surprised, but intrigued as well.

"Toby says we could. There are people, gentry who might have noticed something. Toby can't question them, but, we could, without their even realizing it. Just in the way of conversation. What think you?"

"I think, I am going upstairs and not think about it for the remainder of this evening." Maxie stood up.

"And tomorrow?"

"Tomorrow is another day. We shall just have to wait for it to come."

Freddy watched her glide out of the room. She would help. It was her way.

Chapter Sixteen

Mid-morning found Doctor John's housekeeper, Mrs. Baxley and his cook taking a cup of tea together. Cook leaned over the table and winked. "Seems there is a romance brewing at Huntly and Romney."

"Never say so? Do you mean Miss Claire? For I rather thought little Maxine was sweet on Doctor John?" returned Mrs. Baxley sharply. Then she shrugged. "Though at her age, feelings do change."

Doctor John was just about to enter his kitchen and inform his housekeeper that he would be gone for the remainder of the day. He stopped short outside the kitchen door, his interest held captive by the conversation.

"That do be true, and m'self, I never thought she was more than admiring our doctor, not really in a passion, but tisn't Maxie. Tis Miss Claire."

"You do say?"

"I would if ye would, but, listen," said Cook on a note of frustration. Noting that her friend had pressed her lips together tightly, she hurried on with her news. "I was at market late afternoon yesterday; one of the Romney people was there and we fell to chatting. Seems, the new gentleman at Romney Grange do look as though he be courting Miss Claire. Had a picnic with her and Maxine, he did." Cook said this last with a knowing inclination of her round head.

Doctor John did not like the sound of that. He had quite made up his mind to have Maxine Tarnover for his wife. She was a passionate piece of fluff who would breathe life into his fusty home. She would give him children and she would scribble at her work, earning them money for all the extra luxuries he meant to have. As to Claire, he had some days ago decided she would not do for him. There wasn't any fire in Claire, and he had a need for a woman with hot blood running in her veins!

He wanted no interference. It was worrisome, thinking of Maxie at Romney with the likes of Waremont as Sir Leigh's guest. Waremont's reputation had found it's way to Rye. He would have to have a watchful eye to Maxie.

He really should drive over to pay his respects to his new neighbor. A twinge of jealousy touched his heart. He was not even a direct descendent, merely a cousin. It wasn't fair! No one knew his secret. No one knew what would have been his, should be his. The old bitterness welled up inside of him and filled his heart with fury Damn them! Damn them all! He wouldn't think about it. He couldn't think about it, for it was long ago over and done.

Instead he thought of Claire and his expression moved into a pronounced sneer. She was nought. She had proven herself no better than all of her kind. She had given him every indication that she was intrigued and ready for his courtship, but she had turned to a titled, richer prize. So be it. He had never really wanted Claire.

He frowned as his thoughts began a whirlwind activity. He must now fix his interest with Maxie, before anyone else decided to do so! She was, afterall, a beauty and if he were not careful, he might find a rival in the wings. With this sudden concern on his mind, he walked easily into the kitchen and smiled to say he was riding over to Huntly Grange before he started his rounds.

Cook and Mrs. Baxley watched him leave through the rear kitchen door and then exchanged meaningful glances. Their doctor, they were sure, was going courting!

At that moment Maxie was driving toward Rye, Claire sitting stiffly beside her, with a large basket full of Cook's finest pastries between them. Maxine attempted to change Claire's stiff mood. "We shall be at Tom Bagner's in no time and then you may go about your business in town. I shan't even hold you to a time—"

"I don't see why I must accompany you to Mr. Bagner's. It isn't as if he were one of Papa's tenants. That would be quite a different matter. Calling on one of the tenants after such a dreadful event is expected," complained Claire.

"Event? This was not an event, it was a tragedy," snapped Maxie. "Claire, you do shock me at times. You are not so cold-hearted as that. It is an ugly, ugly sadness this man is faced with. His wife died only a year ago and to lose his daughter in this way. It is our duty as human beings to pay him our heart-felt respects." Maxie's compassion flushed her cheeks.

Claire looked sulky but she sighed in resignation. "Oh, I suppose."

However, when they reached Tom's cottage some ten minutes later, they found the kitchen door open, but, no sign of Tom. Maxie put the basket on the table, then went to leave a message with one of Tom's neighbors. When she returned she saw Claire was looking at an embroidered pot holder bible verse, hanging over the fire place.

"His wife or daughter must have worked that. He must feel so lost, living here with their memory all around," Claire said on a hushed note. "Max, forgive me for being so churlish before. I am quite ashamed of myself."

"It is hard to imagine what is not familiar." Max patted her arm, "Come then, let us do your shopping."

"No, no. How black do you think my heart is? I couldn't, not now."

Quietly they went outdoors and stood a moment at the curbing when a familiar voice at their backs turned their heads.

"Good morning!"

It was Kinnaid. He had spotted Claire and had not been able to stop from calling her attention to himself.

Under his breath, Waremont hissed. "You are behaving like a love-sick fool! What, shall we stroll about the town with them and bump into someone who knows us?"

Claire had by this time discovered that her knees were weak and it was all she could do to stop her feet from racing in his direction. She put up her fingers and wiggled them shyly. He was coming toward her and she smiled a welcome, as she extended her hand to his reaching grasp. "What a pleasant surprise, my lord." Claire said softly.

His response was not heard as he linked her arm through his, pulled her off to the side and spoke softly for her alone. Waremont and Maxie exchanged glances, which resulted in the sounds of his chuckling and her giggles.

"It is priceless to watch Claire behave like a moonstruck miss!" Maxie was shaking her head. "You must know that she has never, ever, behaved so before. She is always so very pragmatic and has claimed that *I* am the romantic. Ha!"

"Well, I can't quite say that about er, my friend." Waremont found he could not look into her violet eyes and call Kinnaid by his own name. "His is a very romantic nature. However, I can say that I have never seen such a concentration of it inflicted upon any other female of our acquaintance." Waremont gazed at her for a long moment. "You are quite ravishing, love. You will slay hearts if you mean to walk about looking so . . . desirable. Are you in town to do some shopping?" It was obvious from their location that they were not, for Tom's cottage was very near the docks and the fish market.

She shook her head and her eyes clouded over. "Came by to . . . pay our respects to Tom Bagner. He wasn't home, so we left a basket. Claire had wanted to do some shopping, but felt it was sadly out of place . . ."

"You surprise me, love. Most young gently-bred women would not feel it came within their realm to pay a tradesman such a visit." He eyed her consideringly.

"Then they are not really gently-bred, at least not in their hearts," returned Maxie without hesitation.

He smiled warmly at her. "So clear-sighted."

She was embarrassed by his scrutiny and moved to change the subject, "And you? What brings you two into town this morning?"

"Tom Bagner," he answered easily. "He was there when we dropped by and we had an informative chat. We of course did not know his poor child, but want to see her murderer punished. We wished him to know that we would do whatever we could to that end."

"Oh. That was so very kind of you . . . and his lordship. You know, he does not fit his reputation at all. For one thing, he is not at all a womanizer, at least from what I can see of him."

"Don't you think so?"

"No, and I shall tell you that I do not miss very

much. Two young, very pretty, serving girls with their skirts hiked up very high, just walked by. He did not even glance in their direction, and it would have been a very natural thing for him, for any man, to have looked their way. However, he did not. He was fully absorbed with my cousin. *You*, on the other hand, though calling me love and telling me how pretty I am, had a very good look at them." There was the tease in her tone and her violet eyes twinkled. She laughed outloud at his startled expression. She was enjoying her bantering play with this man. She could not deny he excited her. She liked the way he responded to her. Everything about him thrilled her, and she had known some very real jealousy when she watched him eye the passing girls.

"Indeed, you must not always believe what you hear," he answered, "and if I glanced at two passing pretties, *my love*, it served to prove to my eye that there is no other as lovely as thee!"

"Oh, bravo!" She clapped saucily. "Well done. You must break hearts with art such as that on your ready tongue." She then allowed her lashes to brush her cheeks, "And, I think I told you once before, *I* am *not* your love."

He answered her softly, "Oh, but, my dear, I thought I made it clear, I should like you to be."

She frowned at him then. "Fie, Sir Leigh, each time you do that, you make it sound more convincing, more natural. However, I am too wise to allow myself to be shamefully seduced." Again her violet eyes glittered naughtily.

"Sadly, I have discovered the truth of that. I am persuaded no man could pull the wool over your eyes."

She sighed. "Poor Anne. Someone played with her feelings. Freddy says that Toby discovered that she had a beau no one knew anything at all about."

"Really? Now that could mean something."

"Yes, both Freddy and Toby seem to think so. I don't see why?"

"Because he was a secret. Secrets sometimes are dangerous things, that is why, pretty Max."

"Yes, secrets are very often cruel things as well," she answered softly. "At any rate, why would this mystery fellow want to kill a sweet girl like Anne? It doesn't make sense to me."

"Why, indeed?" He then looked at her in a way that made her nearly catch her breath. "Perhaps you and I might look into this matter."

"That is what Freddy wants to do." She shook her head. "I suppose if we want Annie's killer found, we can not leave it to Mr. Beadle."

"Then we are agreed. I shall nose about town and see what I can come up with. Perhaps you may know some special friend of Anne's that you could speak to and we will compare notes."

"I shall try. I didn't really know Anne, but I shall try and do what I can." She sighed as she moved away from him to the carriage. "Well, I have kept my horse standing too long already." She turned to Claire. "Are you ready love?" She saw Claire and Lord Waremont move toward the carriage and gave Sir Leigh a smile as she extended her hand.

His blue eyes glittered as he took her gloved hand into both of his and asked softly, "What, love? Do you really expect me to only touch?" He was already bending his head, exposing her wrist, lightly, yet, warmly kissing her flesh.

Maxie felt her body tremble, but her violet eyes flashed at him as she gently pulled away. "I expect that you would not do what you have not been invited to do. That sir, is what I expect."

"Then you mistake your man." He inclined his head as he took her elbow and led her to the open carriage.

Maxie could not believe the boldness of his flirtation. He was a rake! How dare he play his games with her? Well, she had heard stories about London rakes unfeelingly seducing country maids. But, he was out of his quarter if he thought she was nought but a green girl! No doubt he wanted no more than to take her to bed and leave her broken-hearted. Pleasure was all his kind thought about. How could he? Did he have no conscience? What a man like that needed was to be taught a lesson. Indeed, what *he* needed was to be taught a lesson, *by her!*

What would he do if she returned his bold address? Would he be alarmed enough to take a step backward if he thought she was actually stupid enough to think he was really in earnest? Or would this self-assured, arrogant blade *still* try and take her to bed? After all, she was not some poor country serving girl without any protection? Maxie's mind set as she put her foot up to the first step and turned to him to smile invitingly. "Oh, my dear sir . . . I don't think so." Now her violet eyes were twinkling adorably and there was the suggestion of something unnamed in the look. "I am quite sure I have your measure. The thing is . . . I don't think you have mine." She gave him her back and continued to take the steps to the carriage bench.

Chapter Seventeen

Doctor John was not in a sunny mood. Peltons had met him at the door of Huntly Grange with the intelligence that Miss Claire and Miss Maxine had gone to town. Further prompting won him no other information. He hadn't the time to spare and couldn't go chasing after Maxie everywhere she went. He was very irritated. Hell and Brimstone! The girl never stayed put. What did she have to do in town every other day? Her restlessness was something he would most certainly curb when they were wed. He frowned over the problem. Well, it just happened that two of his calls were patients living in town. He had planned a visit to these patients later in the day. No matter, he would just rearrange his schedule.

He arrived just as Waremont was handing Maxie up to her carriage. A silent rage swept through the doctor's lean body as he watched their flirtatious exchange. He pulled on the reins abruptly and commanded his cob to settle down as it objected to the rough handling. He was attempting to calm his temper as Maxie brought her vehicle up so that she sat just opposite. He could see from the corner of his eye that the two gentlemen standing in the roadway were still looking after Maxie's carriage. He looked away from them. He was nearly out of control.

Maxie beamed happily as she pulled her carriage horse to a stop, "Good morning, Doctor John." She arched a teasing look his way.

"It certainly is now," he said mustering up a smile. Then he asked almost indulgently, "Shopping all done?"

Maxie sighed. "Ah, a man thinks a woman has nought to do in town but shop. Frivolous beings, that is all we are, Claire." The tease was there and it lit in her eyes.

He laughed. "Now, Maxine, you *know* that I know better." He was, of course, referring to Maxie's writing career.

"Indeed, I *thought* so," Maxie returned banteringly.

"Oh now stop, both of you!" laughed Claire. "We were on an errand of mercy. We dropped by poor Mr. Bagner's cottage." She shook her head. "It is such an awful, ugly ordeal for the unhappy man."

"Yes it is, but, though you were most kind to do so, it was completely unnecessary."

Maxie frowned at him as she retorted, "Unnecessary? I am not certain what that means? You of all people know that acts of kindness are vital. It is what characterizes us as human beings." She arched a look at him. "You are the first to rush out to someone's aid, regardless of his ability to pay you for the service."

"Maxie, Maxie . . . always giving as good as you get,

eh? You are a treasure." He said this last softly and his eyes moved to her lips.

Maxie blushed beneath the intensity of his gaze. "Ah, but, Doctor John, I can sight you many instances when you did not think so."

"Even when you were at your worst, you were a treasure to me. I thought you knew that, Maxine." His voice was soft, caressing. He could feel Claire staring, but a large part of him wanted to punish Miss Claire Huntly; to show her what she was losing. Even more than that did he want Claire to know that he had never any real serious intention of making her his bride. Thus, he was prompted to add, "That in mind, don't you think it time you called me by my given name?"

She smiled affectionately, "Why, so you have always been, dear Doctor . . . John."

He saw her retreat in her eyes and immediately changed back into friend with a short chuckle. "Just so. Now, before I let you go, tell me, for I am embarrassed to say that I have not yet, had the time to pay a call at Romney Grange; was that the new owner and his houseguest I noticed chatting with you just moments ago?" He sighed over the possibility. "I hope they don't mean to leave the Grange before I have had a chance to ride over and welcome Sir Leigh."

"I suppose you must do so before long," said Max ruefully. "For I don't think Rye will keep them from London many more days."

"Don't you think so?" Claire frowned at Maxine. "His lordship gave no indication to *me* that they would be leaving any day soon." It was quite obvious that the notion disturbed her greatly.

"Ah, well . . . who is to say?" She turned to the doctor. "We must not keep you from your patients and as we are due home to do . . . oh, all the things that *females* must do." She teased with her eyes as she arched a look at him over her dainty shoulder.

The doctor laughed and tipped his hat to her. "A flush hit, I must count myself properly set-down."

"Oh, only a very little." Maxie beamed, happy to be back on steady ground. With a snap of the reins, she started her horse forward.

He smiled as he waved them off, but his smile was a mere parting of the lips. He was in a rage. He was irritated beyond reason. He made excuses for Maxie's sudden aloofness. She was still young, even, perhaps unprepared as yet, for his courtship. This was something he had been willing to take slowly, tenderly encouraging her to his suit, but, now all that was changed. Here were two London rakes hovering and Maxie was an ingenue, easy prey!

He would not stand for their interference! It had already gone to Claire's head. Why, the girl certainly appeared besotted by that rake Waremont? He didn't want these men working their talents on Maxie's innocent character. And, the thing was that she was most certainly an innocent, he told himself. Even in her wildest scrapes, she was ever honest, pure, different from all her kind . . .

Damnation! Why couldn't the London roués just return to their sordid haunts and pleasures in the city that boasted all their kind? He hated them, oh, how he hated them!

Claire gave Maxie a look and then commented caustically, "Well, I must say *he* has managed to astound me!"

"What do you mean?" returned Maxie though she knew full well just what her cousin was saying.

"No, no don't play off your gammon with me. I may be gullible to many of your games Max, but, you know full well what I mean though in truth it is difficult to put into words."

Maxie incurably honest sighed. "You noticed? Don't look at me like that, I know you noticed. The thing is, I don't feel that way about Doctor John."

"Good. I am very glad to hear it," announced Claire with a humph.

"You are? Why?" Maxie was surprised.

"Because I have just seen your precious Doctor John in a new light and Maxie it was not at all flattering."

"What the devil are you talking about?" ejaculated Maxine in shocked accents.

"You must learn to curb your tongue Maxie. Swearing is not at all becoming in a woman."

"Never mind that, tell me what you are talking about now."

"My dear cousin, apparently your good doctor means to toy with us. I can see it all so clearly. He always made a point of calling on me when you were not at home. Of course, he hadn't made up his mind which one of us he would have."

"That is a gothic story," laughed Maxie, "You saw how he behaved just now? Has he suddenly decided to have *me?*" She shook her head. "Why?"

"I don't know. Max, you must have noticed that he would scarcely look at me just now. It was almost as though he wanted me to see him openly make you the object of his strenuous attentions and, Max, you can not deny that he was somewhat brazen."

Maxie frowned. "I don't understand any of this. Are you telling me that Doctor John has been courting you, Claire? You never said a word?"

Claire gave a half-smile. "Well, in truth, I didn't know just how I felt about him. He was far more interesting and attractive than any of the young men of our acquaintance and I suppose I was flattered." She looked away from Max. "Now of course, I know precisely what a woman should feel for a man before she marries him and it wasn't what I felt for Doctor John."

"Aha! So, you know, eh? How do you know? No, don't tell me. I am not blind. You are in love with Waremont. Faith, I don't know whether to be happy for you or go and shoot the man dead."

"*Maxie!*" objected Claire and then she giggled. "Oh Max ... I think he ... I have the notion that he feels the same."

"Do you? Well, but, you are just a country girl, not up to snuff, you know. He is a London beau with a reputation for being a rake. You could be easily fooled by such as he."

"Oh no, Maxie, no!" Claire clutched at Maxie's arm and looked so shaken that Maxine relented.

"There, there . . . what do I know? If I were you and following my instincts, they would tell me that this time, this time Rake Waremont was in earnest."

Claire sighed. "Oh, Max."

Chapter Eighteen

It didn't take long for Kinnaid to conclude his business with his solicitor and for him and Waremont to make their way to the Mermaid Inn. As they entered the public room Waremont noticed a large fisherman and with a signal to Kinnaid moved toward the older fellow.

"Captain Toby? You don't know me, but I know of you. Apparently, you are held in some esteem by Frederick Huntly and his cousin, Miss Maxine Tarnover."

"Well now, I own m'own ship, but, m'men jest call me Toby. I think it will serve ye as well," said Toby matter of factly. "As to young Freddy and Miss Maxie, what's yer point?"

Waremont liked him at once. He smiled and felt a sudden rapport with the weathered seaman. "I should like to get to that in my own good time. Would you take a bumper of ale with us?"

"Now, I don't know. Who would I be drinking wit?"

Waremont grinned. "I'm Lord Waremont, and my

friend here is Sir Leigh of Romney Grange. Will that do for you?"

"Bless ye. Whot would ye be wanting wit the loikes of me?"

Waremont looked round and indicated a round table in the far corner. "Where we might be private, if you please?"

Toby nodded and moved to take up a chair with his back to the wall and his eye to an exit.

Waremont noted this and chuckled. "We mean to be friends, not foes, Toby. You see, we visited Tom this morning and have a notion to help you find his daughter's murderer."

"Eh, then, be ye larking?" He shook his head, "This be serious business. Someone else could be 'urt. A killer, well now, 'ee won't taike kindly to anyone creeping up on 'im, will 'ee?"

"Yet you mean to stalk him, don't you, sir?" asked Kinnaid with a frown. "Why should we be any less principled than yourself?"

"Ye 'ave more to lose," said Toby practically.

"Toby, there is a murderer walking about freely. He believes that he has taken the life of a young woman and is free to do so again. There is something to lose in that," answered Waremont gravely. "Now, shall we put our heads together and divvy up our time and our resources?"

"Right then. I'll be trusting ye wit this. Annie 'ad a friend whot could 'elp us fer tis almost certain she knew who Annie was seeing. 'Er name be Sarah Jane Stone and she be *missing!*"

* * *

By the time Doctor John had made his calls, he was weary and strangely frenzied. He left his cart at the livery and marched toward the Mermaid Inn. Before he entered he looked at its Tudor façade and hesitated. What was he doing at the Mermaid? He didn't ordinarily patronize this establishment. Still, he found himself entering its portals. He quickly discovered Waremont, Kinnaid and Toby! His brow went up. Now, there was a strange trio.

He had no sooner received his tankard of ale than he saw the three men get to their feet and shake hands. He was amazed. What the deuce was this? Toby moved toward the rear exit, but Kinnaid and Waremont passed by Doctor John. He managed an amiable smile as he locked glances with Waremont. "Hallo. May I intrude a moment and introduce myself. I am Doctor John Wiltshire, and you are, I believe, Sir Leigh Kinnaid?"

To his surprise, the other man pushed forward and put out his hand. "I am Kinnaid and this is my very good friend, Lord Waremont."

The doctor was momentarily diverted for he had it in his mind that it was the other way around. However, no matter. It was time to make his move. "May I invite you to join me?" He raised his tankard.

"Thank you, we have some pressing business, but perhaps you might enjoy joining us for dinner one evening soon?" answered Sir Leigh.

"Indeed, I should like that, but I had rather thought you two would have found Rye sadly lacking by now."

Waremont answered. "You are out there, Doctor. Rye has a great deal to offer"—and then in another tone altogether, one the doctor was sure he understood—"a great deal."

The doctor smiled and watched them take their leave. Damn them to perdition! So, Waremont had laid down his cards. He meant to have Maxine? Did he think so? Did he really think so?

Maxie found Freddy standing on the dock throwing pieces of bread to Cyg. She called out to him and ran the remainder of the way cooing to Cyg all the while. She had a basket of day-old buns for the young swan and laughed as she greeted her cousin. "Ah, we are of a same mind, you and I."

He grinned at her. "I came here to see if Cyg had any answers for me."

She knew what he was talking about and from the gravity of his face, she knew he had come to a decision. She was nearly afraid to ask. "Did he?"

"Brilliant swan, you know. Trusts you. Said I should trust you as well. I think he is right. I shall enter Cambridge," he said on a grim note.

Maxie threw back her head with a happy laugh and then threw both her arms round him. "Oh Freddy-boy, you shall never regret it."

"If I do, you will as well," he grinned at her, and then shrugged. "There are one or two things they might be able to teach me over there."

"Hmmm. One or two." She laughed and then tossed

a bun to Cyg who was waiting patiently. "We didn't see Tom Bagner this morning. He wasn't in when we got there."

"Aye, he said something yesterday about walking Winchelsea way."

"Really? Does he think the magistrate there might be able to help?" Max's interest was perked. "It is a good notion to poke about there, I think."

"No, he hasn't the heart just now to go poking about. He wanted to speak with Anne's priest."

"Anne's *priest?* Whatever do you mean?"

"Tom is Protestant, but Anne chose to follow the Catholic religion like her mother. Anne's mother was Irish."

Suddenly Maxie's eyes lit up, "Never say so!" She took his hand. "Come on Freddy, we must saddle up as fast as we can."

"What? What the devil are you at now?" he asked in some surprise.

"We are going to pay Anne's priest a visit as well, and we will have no problem poking around, will we?"

"By Jove, Max, what a famous notion!" he said picking up on her enthusiasm.

Chapter Nineteen

The ride back to Romney Grange was done for the most part in silence. Finally Waremont broke the tension. "Right then, Leigh! Don't fester, speak your mind. You always do in the end, so we might as well get on with it."

"We are in the suds," said Leigh gloomily. "She thinks I am Lord Waremont. She is an angel, a divine creature and I have played her false." His shoulders sagged. "I am the very lowest form of life." he glanced at his friend. "No, the second lowest. *You* wear the crown in this!"

"Oh stubble it!" Waremont was himself feeling like a cad, but he, unlike Kinnaid had already come to a decision. "It is out of our hands now. Toby knows who we are, the good Doctor John knows who we are and at any rate, I had every intention of confessing our duplicity to Mr. Huntly before we returned to London." He sighed ruefully. "Now, we shall just have to do so immediately."

Kinnaid swiveled so hard on his horse that he nearly fell off. "What? Upon my soul! We can't do that. She will hate me for all eternity."

"At least she will know the true name of the man she is hating," said Waremont who had no patience with this style of thinking. He was the sort of man who took things head-on.

"Seth, Seth . . . we can not."

"We can, and we shall, Leigh. I have been thinking so for days," said Waremont gravely. "I have led you into this bobbery of ours, but I shall not enact the coxcomb and continue it. It is no longer a game."

Kinnaid sighed. "Damnation, I have always been man enough to make my own decisions. You presented a lark and *I* decided to go along with it. Consequences, consequences . . . they are mine as well as yours. The truth is that I have always enjoyed switching identities with you, Seth, but in the past we were really no more than lads. It hurt no one, at least, I must hope that it did not." He shook his head, "I may have moaned and groaned over *this* lark, but you certainly didn't lead me anywhere I didn't wish to go." He stared ahead blankly and said on a soulful note, "My life is over."

"Blister it, man! Such halfling cries over a woman?" Waremont grimaced. "Spare me that, at least. It is our honor we have undone. And this time, Leigh, I don't see how we shall come about?"

Waremont himself was feeling despondent over what the future held. Max had told him that secrets were very often cruel things. She would certainly have no doubt about that now. Maxie with her openness would hold

him in contempt. Why shouldn't she? What was wrong
with him? Why had he ever pulled such a trick on the
Huntlys? Looking back on it now, he found it unforgivable. Damnation! How was he to know they would stay
on at Romney so long? They were to have left within a
few days, long before any friendship had taken place.
Long before he had learned to appreciate a little minx
of a woman called Maxine Tarnover!

He thought of Maxie's smile. Her features came viv-
idly to mind. Thunder and Turf! Well, there was no
doubt now. Maxie Tarnover would never smile at him
again. She probably would never even look at him, and
the notion vexed him sorely.

St. Mary's Church was on a country road between
Rye and Winchelsea. After getting lost for more than
ten minutes, and engaging in a strong debate that
wasted another few minutes, Max and Freddy discovered the steeple of the church with its simple cross loom-
ing in the blue sky like a beacon. With a thankful cry,
they followed its direction and within only a few minutes
were tethering their horses outside the church. Maxie
had ridden sidesaddle and was complaining that her
right leg was feeling numb.

Freddy snorted. "Whats this, whats this? It is an easy
thing to do. That's why we men designed it for women."

"Easy, is it? Right then, *you* try it. I should like to see
you jump a fence with both legs on one side of a horse."

He put up his chin. "Bet that I could."

"Ah, a wager is it? What then?"

Freddy really did not want to take this particular feat on. He shrugged his shoulders hoping that she would forget the matter if he put it aside. "We'll see. Now, we have more important things to attend to."

Maxie eyed her cousin superiorly. "Humph!" She then swept past him and took the flagstone steps that led to the church porch. They were met there by an elderly gentleman with a great cloud of fluffy white hair framing a pink face. His smile was soft and his green eyes were bright and warm. Maxie liked him immediately. After they exchanged introductions, she felt momentarily unsure of just how she could phrase her questions, and hurriedly began, "Father McRay, we can see you are on your way out and shan't keep you long—"

Father McRay believed in direct speaking. He prompted her with a twinkling eye. "You rode all the way here from Huntly, so do indeed, keep me. How is it that I may help you?"

"How good of you to notice that we are in need of help. I am very nearly sure that when Tom Bagner was here this morning, about Anne, he did not have the spirit to ask the sort of questions whose answers might lead to finding her murderer." Maxie's violet eyes implored him to understand.

He formed a pyramid with his two hands and pressed his lips to its tip while he thought for a moment. When he regarded Maxie again it was to ask sadly, "And what answers do you think *I* might have?"

"Anne was a Catholic. You were her priest. She must have come to you, in confidence, I know, during confession."

"If you know that much, young lady, then you know Anne's confessions are her own. I could not betray her in life or death." Father McRay was very grave.

"I do know that. However, I am not asking you to repeat anything she actually told you."

"Are you not? What then are you asking?"

"You knew her, heard her confessions, perhaps understood her better than anyone else, wouldn't you say?"

"Perhaps. What are you getting at, child?"

"Did you know, not from confession, but from friendship, if there was some special man, Anne was in love with, someone no one else knew about?"

He pulled himself erect. "I shall have to think about this." He shook his head. "The child is dead. I don't want her name or anyone else's besmirched because of idle gossip."

"We don't want to hear about gossip. We want only what you know to be a fact, and you *do* know. You would have seen things because you saw them through her eyes, because you knew of her joys, her woes. I am not asking you to betray the principles of the confessional, I only want to know what you saw." Maxine spoke deliberately.

"Indeed, even what we see is not always truth. I will give this a great deal of thought."

"And after you have wrestled with your thoughts, will you send us word at Huntly Grange?" Maxie asked hopefully.

Freddy had been watching this exchange in some fascination. "Please, Father," he added quietly.

"Yes, I will do that. But, tell me something. What has this ugly affair to do with you two? You are children yourselves."

"A young woman was murdered, brutally, without care. It has to do with all of us, Father," answered Maxie grimly.

"Aye, then. I shall answer you as soon as I may." As Max extended her hand, he took it and said gravely, "There is something you might want to look into in the meantime."

"What is that?" Maxie puzzled up at him.

"Our Doctor Wrenfield here in Winchelsea made an examination of poor Anne's body. He made his report to your magistrate, Mr. Beadle."

"Yes?" Freddy frowned as if he did not understand what the priest was implying.

"It is my humble opinion that his report is very important. Something that deserves attention immediately. The doctor and I have a notion that Mr. Beadle merely shoved the thing into a drawer."

"Right then," said Freddy. "The doctor's report."

Maxie eyed the gentle priest thoughtfully. "Are you telling us that something so vital to finding a vicious killer was ignored by the authorities? How can this be?"

"Sometimes the local authorities feel they don't have the time for a fisherman's daughter. It is a sorry fact."

"You feel there might be a clue in this report?" asked Freddy in some excitement.

"I do, however, it isn't for me to say. I am in the business of healing souls." He then added, "But, if I *were* trying to do the job you have taken on, yes, I would say that report is vital."

A moment later Father McRay took his leave of them. Freddy and Max stopped just as they untethered their horses and exchanged meaningful glances before breathing in one voice, *"Zounds!"*

Mr. Huntly had heard the two gentlemen out in stoic and what they assumed was a virulent silence, boding ill. This was what they had expected, and therefore, neither Waremont nor Kinnaid was surprised when Mr. Huntly put both his hands at his back and turned away from them.

Kinnaid began fidgeting, touching his neatly tied cravat, clearing his throat and looking like a wayward boy. Lord Waremont had himself discovered that he was deeply ashamed, but was well able to keep the blush from his cheeks. He regarded his friend and raised a brow in an effort to deter what he felt was unseemly and unmanly behavior. He knew himself a cad, but he meant to take his punishment with noble resolve. He returned his attention to Mr. Huntly's back when he noted with some surprise that the man's shoulders appeared to be shaking. Huntly's hand went to his face as he turned round to address them in a tone they did not quite understand. "Then it was Sir Leigh who invited my daughter and Maxine to enjoy a romp around Romney Grange and a picnic my wife is still in raptures over?"

"I am sorry to say that yes, we carried on with the charade even then. We deeply regret our unpardonable behavior." Waremont attempted to apologize, but was cut off by a bark of a laughter. Both Kinnaid and Waremont watched in some disbelief as Mr. Huntly's mirth seemed beyond his control. They continued to watch as Huntly wiped at his eyes and bade them be seated and comfortable. Waremont and Kinnaid exchanged doubtful glances pregnant with wonder, but they took up two leather upholstered wing chairs as their host sank into his own behind his desk and faced them.

Waremont managed to find his voice as he regarded his host. "Sir, I don't think we quite understand your . . . er, reaction to our thoughtless prank."

"Do you not? Well, but you should. You must remember I am married to just the sort of woman who prompted you to trade identities. No doubt, my lord, you were merely trying to discharge an errand for your lovely mother. Knowing there was a marriageable daugher in our household you chose to escape another tiresome bombardment of female entrapments. Oh, I have never been the object of such attentions, but, it is not a thing I envy you and I sympathize with your repulsion. I hold no grudge, indeed, as you have witnessed, I am appreciative of the humor of your game. It is a jest my wife well deserves." He went on with a wave of his hand, "Finding that your residence here in Rye was being prolonged, you did the honorable thing and acknowledged your crime to me. I forgive you, nay, I applaud you." He shook his head. "My wife has been driving me mad. She has accused me of being in the way. She told me last night, only last night, that if I allowed our daughter a London Season, she would have no trouble securing her a noble duke for a husband, if Claire had so easily captivated Rake Waremont! Ha!"

"Then you do not hold us in contempt?" asked Kinnaid hopefully.

"No, no I do not . . . er . . . Sir Leigh, however, when my daughter and Maxine discover your duplicity, well, there will be some hell to pay, mark me in this. A shame, but women are never very understanding of such things, are they?"

"No." Kinnaid sighed. "And perhaps this is not the moment to bring this up, but, well . . . the thing is . . . I should like, that is . . . if you allow, I want to . . ."

Mr. Huntly smiled benignly. "I know, you wish to court my girl, Claire?"

"Yes," breathed Kinnaid, pleased to find Mr. Huntly had such a ready grasp of matters.

"That is quite another thing, is it not?"

"You mean that Mrs. Huntly will object?" Kinnaid hung his head.

"No, no." Mr. Huntly chuckled. "I mean to tell Mrs. Huntly that she has been mistaken from the start. That we often tried to correct her, but she never listened because she was too busy talking, talking, always talking!" He sighed with great satisfaction. "That should shut her up for a bit!"

"What then, do you think is my obstacle?" Kinnaid pursued.

Waremont stared at him in disbelief before sneering, "What the blazes do think is your obstacle? You have been making a cake of yourself over Miss Huntly but

your name was a lie, a bold-faced lie. You will be lucky
if she doesn't cut you dead the next time you try and
speak to her!" He didn't know if Claire's principles were
such that she would really do more than give his friend
a set-down, but deep inside he knew Maxine would find
his behavior unforgivable. "I doubt that Miss Huntly or
Miss Tarnover will ever speak to us again!"

"Yes, but Claire is so kind . . . so good, might she not
be forgiving?" Kinnaid asked hopefully looking to Mr.
Huntly for his answer.

"Women are mysterious creatures. Who is to say what
they will forgive, and what they will not?" was all Mr.
Huntly was willing to say on that subject.

As Waremont and Kinnaid rode down the drive, they
met Max coming toward them.

"I am so glad you are here," she told Waremont and
smiled at Kinnaid. "I have so much to tell you!"

Waremont was uncomfortably aware of his lie. Her
face was that of a beautiful ingenue. How could such as
she understand what he had done? It was difficult to
meet her gaze and he knew he should stop her and immediately confess his sin, but he had promised Kinnaid
that they would take on the task with both girls together.

"So much, eh? What then, love?"

She glared at him. "I don't have time to scold you,
but recall, I am not your love." She looked to Kinnaid.
"You must instruct your friend in the proprieties, I
think."

"Acquit me, he is beyond my scope."

Maxie laughed. "I discovered something today, I did

not know before." This last was said portentiously, excitedly.

"And what is that, my monkey?" teased Waremont. He found her in every single way, more adorable than any woman he had ever known.

Maxie needed no more prompting before she lunged in "It seems that Annie was an Irish Catholic, like her mother, and she worshipped at St. Mary's in Winchelsea!" Waremont's blue eyes glittered appreciatively at her as he released a low whistle. However, he took an authorative stance and frowning said, "And of course, you rode right over there. I hope not by yourself."

She waved off this objection, "No, no Freddy was with me. He's has gone to tell Captain Toby. You will never guess why we went?"

"I rather think you went to ask her priest to betray the confessional," said Waremont thoughtfully. "Which I trust, he refused to do."

A little daunted she shrugged her shoulders. "Well, yes . . . but I questioned him about her from a different point of view. I told him that I wanted to know what he might have seen and better understood because he was her priest, her friend. I asked him if he had ever seen anything that might help us discover who her killer might be."

"Did you, by Jove? Good girl!" Kinnaid said.

Waremont smiled fondly. "And?"

"He promised to give it deep consideration for he does not want to injure an innocent person by repeating what might not be pertinent." She reached out and touched Waremont's arm. "But there is more!"

He found her touch thrilled him beyond reason. He discovered her violet eyes alive with her excitement and he was touched by the sudden tenderness she seemed to draw from a soul he had thought long ago destroyed. "More? Egad, woman . . . what more?" He was teasing, and saw at once that she was offended by his easy, light attitude. She would not be treated like a child. He suddenly wanted, almost needed to scoop her out of her saddle and take her into his arms. He wanted desperately to hold her, touch her lips. He wanted to . . . Stop! This just had to stop! Bloody Hell! What was wrong with him? She was just a chit of a girl. Too young, too green, far too wonderful for such as he! He was a jaded rake and she was but an innocent child.

Up went her nose. "Oh well, if you are going to poke fun, perhaps, you are not the one I should be coming to with—"

He cut her off. "I am the *only* one you should come to . . . always."

She blushed and regarded her gloved fingers before proceeding with her news. "Well, Father McRay told us the village doctor made initial examination of poor Anne. He said the report was given to Mr. Beadle, but Father McRay doesn't think Mr. Beadle has bothered much about it, for some reason. Father McRay believes the report is vital. That is the word he used, *vital,* " said Maxie, once again bubbling with sure excitement.

"Devilish queer doings," commented Kinnaid doubtfully.

"Good work, little one," said Waremont thoughtfully. He turned to Kinnaid. "Well, you know then, where we are off to now, don't you?"

"You are going to Beadle, aren't you? Good. Freddy and I weren't quite sure if he would show us the medical report, but I don't suppose he would dare deny *you* access to it." She regarded him shyly.

"Yes, my love. See how recalcitrant I am, continuing to call you that which you are to me?" Why was he dallying with her so boldly? It was as though he couldn't stop himself. This was not his style. He did not toy with young innocents.

She giggled deliciously. "Stop it, you dreadful wretch. Right then, off you go, but, do please send me word?"

"Indeed, I shall and in person, if I may?" He smiled warmly at her.

"You may, and perhaps I may have more news for you as well."

"I tell you what it is, you two weary a fellow with your antics. Here I am being dragged all over the countryside. Should not Tom Bagner or Toby go after this doctor's report?" asked Kinnaid.

"I doubt that Mr. Beadle would give it to Toby even if Toby dared to call upon him," said Maxie eyeing him disapprovingly. "poor Tom as you well know, my lord, is simply not up to such an ordeal."

Kinnaid cringed and retreated into silence. Max noted the sudden sagging of his shoulders and frowned. She seemed about to speak but Waremont took her attention once more, by laughing as he took her gloved fingers into his firm grasp. "Depend on it, little one, we will meet tomorrow."

A moment later, she was waving them off and watching their backs as they left her to trot off down the driveway. Waremont turned suddenly and audaciously threw her a kiss.

Chapter Twenty

Toby regarded Freddy as the boy regaled him with his news. When he had done, Freddy waited expectantly for Toby's reaction to what he felt was something of a major clue in Anne Bagner's murder. He was, therefore, much surprised to find Toby surveying him doubtfully. "Never mind that, lad. There be somethin' else ye and I must be talking about now!"

"How can you put it off like that? Toby, this is important, or at the very least it could be." Freddy was frowning.

"Look 'ere. I ain't no gapeseed. Did ye think I wouldn't find out?"

"Find out? Find out what? Blister it, Toby, what are you talking about?"

"Don't ye trust me? I was 'oping ye would trust me and tell me yerself." Toby was slumped on a pile of line, looking greatly troubled.

"Have you gone daft, Toby?"

"Daft is it?" Toby became incensed. "Why don't ye

tell me whot ye and poor young Anne were all about? Tell me, then!" he snapped and, not waiting for Freddy's reply added, "Ye know we been trying to find out who she was sweet on, and all this time you kept mum!"

"Me? What the deuce are you saying?" Freddy was round-eyed. "I have never been Annie's beau. Toby, what makes you say so?"

"Ye were seen wit the girl. One of m'men seen ye kissing 'er full on her lips. Never blabbed because 'ee never thought much on it."

"Toby, I was never Anne's beau, never! Six, maybe five months ago, I stole a kiss from her when I was down on the quay. She slapped me soundly and gave me a rare trimming. That was the start and the end of it."

Toby accepted this at once and breathed a sigh of relief. His hand went to his heart, and he announced as he dismissed the matter, "There now, knew there was nought to it but I needed you to say so." Then he eyed him slyly. "I was thinking ye didn't 'ave a 'ead yet fer women! Well now, I tell ye lad, ye do keep surprising me, I'll say that fer yer."

"Right then. So, now what do you think will be in the medical report?" asked Freddy returning to the subject at hand. "Do you think Sir Leigh and Lord Waremont will be able to get Old Beadle do-nothing to hand it over to them?"

"Aye, I do."

"Maxie says they will have a better chance of getting it from him than either of us."

"Maxie is right. She 'as a good 'ead on 'er shoulders," agreed Toby.

"Oh, as to that, Maxie is prime to every twig. Knows what she is about and"—Freddy winked—"she didn't think *you* wanted to pay Beadle a visit."

Toby sniffed and raised an eyebrow at Freddy's grinning face. "Lord love ye, that be a right smart girl!"

"You don't think he will give Lord Waremont or Sir Leigh any trouble over it, do you?"

"Bless ye lad, me, I don't think any man would give Waremont any trouble over anything, mark me on that!"

Maxie awoke with a start and touched her forehead. She had been dreaming. Dreaming? She didn't have dreams. She suffered nightmares, terrible on-going nightmares. She felt nearly weary and very troubled. Something was nagging at her, something she felt, sensed, knew and yet, could not grasp. It was there, in Sir Leigh's blue eyes every single time he looked at her, there was something unspoken and it had nought to do with romance. It was something else. There was something that just didn't fit. Her nightmare had her waltzing with him, had him holding her, kissing her and then he was gone. In his place was a darkly clad man holding a length of seaman's line and he was moving towards her. She had wanted to scream, but instead she woke up.

She looked toward the window for she had not drawn

the curtains, and made a face. It was grey and drizzling. Drat! Double drat.

A scratch sounded at her door and as she called out a welcome, Claire put in her head. "Max, we have to talk." So stating she rushed in and sat on the edge of her cousin's bed. "Max, there is something odd going on!"

"Faith, so you feel it too?" Maxie was surprised.

"Well, I don't know *what* you can mean for you have not been up and about yet and have not encountered Papa, but I tell you he is not quite himself this morning. I can't describe it, but he is being secretive, and laughing over nought. And wait till you hear what he said."

"Oh, no doubt he and your mother have bumped heads again over some nonsense." Maxie answered on a smile.

"No, it isn't that at all. Mama has gone to Hastings and won't return until dinner. I had forgotten to mention . . . well, yesterday in town, outside Tom Bagner's, Lord Waremont was kind enough to invite us to join him for a little luncheon at the Sweet Shop—"

She would have gone on, but Maxie interrupted her to raise a brow and level a teasing glance her way. "Another luncheon? My, my."

"Oh Max, do you think it very forward of me for I accepted his invitation?"

"Very forward and very right." Max smiled and then urged, "Go on, go on."

"Well I went to Papa in his study and told him that you and I (I did take it for granted that you would not object to the plan)"—she eyed her cousin warily, received a rueful smile and proceeded—"well, that we were invited to have a luncheon with Lord Waremont in town." She stopped then for breath and then asked, "Do you know what he said?"

"He said, go, eat, enjoy with my blessing." Max laughed. "Uncle is so very easy."

Claire shook her head. "But that isn't what he said."

"You mean we are forbidden the Sweet Shop?" Max put the back of her hand to her forehead in mock dismay.

"Maxie, he said to me 'Lord Waremont? What does he look like?' I answered him, 'Papa, you remember, Lord Waremont. He had dinner with us just recently?' He said to me, 'Ah, but one never knows, does one.' Max, then he burst into laughter and said, 'I have one on her, finally, I have one!' "

"Well, I must say, that is very strange, but you know Claire, there is never any saying how my uncle will behave after he has had a bit of a tiff with your mother," said Maxie frowning over the problem.

"Well, I am worried," returned Claire on a troubled note. "What shall we do?"

"Take the coach, for it is raining," said Max pragmatically.

"Oh do be serious," returned Claire, with her hands on her hips.

"I am being serious. How would it look if we came in the open gig, our bonnets and pretty ensembles soaked through? No, no, the coach!" Maxie tossed a pillow at her cousin as Claire screeched. "Don't you dare!" She ran toward the door, then she stopped to advise her cousin caustically, "For a rough and tumble piece right out of a gothic romance, you are boringly pragmatic, Maxine Tarnover!" As another pillow came flying through the air, Claire quickly ducked into the hall.

Maxie sat back on her bed after her door was closed. She had teased Claire only to keep her from dwelling on her father's odd behavior, but she, too, was startled by it all. This confirmed her suspicion that all was not quite as it seemed!

Freddy had left the house before anyone was up and about. He wasn't ready for Maxie to question him. He had forgotten all about his attempt to kiss Annie Bagner until Toby's reminder yesterday. Maxie would be furious with him for not mentioning the incident. She would say that everyone now will think he was Annie's beau since he was the only one who had been seen kissing her. He wasn't so green that he didn't see the danger in this new development. He wasn't so naive that he didn't know the sure implications, for people who had little to chew on were very likely to grab at scraps!

If he didn't do something, and quickly, his reputation and that of his family would be utterly sullied. Zounds, what would Maxie say? It was mortifying. He just had to set things right. This time, he must not make a mull of it. This time, somehow he had to walk out clean, mature and more like a hero. He had to find Sarah Jane Stone!

He wielded his horse while his wild thoughts played mad havoc with his mind. He knew just where he might get some information on Sarah Jane Stone for though no one knew it, he had once driven her to visit a friend near Lydd. By Jupiter! It suddenly occurred to him that if anything had happened to Sarah, he could be blamed for that as well. This was getting frightening!

Perhaps, just perhaps, he should tell Toby? No. Toby would call him a damn fool and send him home. Toby would take the direction from him and probably not even allow him to come along for the ride. Well, that wasn't fair! He wouldn't be so ill-treated. This was his adventure. This was his problem and this time he would handle it on his own.

Waremont and Sir Leigh walked into Beadle's small and cluttered library where the fellow's obsequious behavior made them uncomfortable. Waremont cut the fellow short and advised him that they were not on a social visit. This seemed to deflate the fat little man who took up a seat behind his desk and asked in some surprise, "Is it not? Why then, are you here?" Beadle took up a miniature confection, eyed it, and then dropped it in his mouth.

Sir Leigh noted that his friend was about to return a caustic answer and hurried in to say, "We are here on behalf of Tom Bagner."

"Really? I can't imagine what you, Sir Leigh, or Lord Waremont could possibly—"

"We are not interested in your imagination," stuck in Waremont who was of the opinion that the fellow was a toad. He had little patience with such as he. "What we want is for you to produce the medical report given to you by the doctor in Winchelsea."

Mr. Beadle may have been offended. However, Waremont's aura of authority left him nervous, too nervous to do more than hurriedly pull open his center drawer to say, "Well, I have it right here. I was scanning it myself only this morning to see if there was anything in it that might shed light on this terrible affair."

Waremont took the offered document and read quickly. It didn't take him long to see why the priest had wanted Maxie to have the report read. He looked up and eyed Beadle contemptuously,

"You scanned this and found nothing?"

"I am sorry to say—" Beadle was shaking his head gravely.

"Then you are an even worse incompetent than I had hitherto assumed!" snapped Waremont who then gave the report to his friend.

Sir Leigh surveyed the page quickly and came up to release a low whistle. He eyed Waremont who had restlessly gotten to his feet. "By Thunder, Seth! This changes everything."

"Precisely so."

Chapter Twenty-One

It had stopped raining. Maxie had a little time to herself before she was due to accompany Claire to town for her luncheon with Waremont. She wondered if Sir Leigh would join them. She was feeling a dangerous attraction for the man, for his blue eyes his charming smile. This was so unlike the level-headed person she knew herself to be. He was a wild London rake. That was all he was. She must remember that. Yet, a very vivid picture of his face seemed to haunt her everywhere she went. That was why she had chosen her blue traveling ensemble and paid detailed attention to her hair before donning her pretty blue silk bonnet. Dark curling bangs and curls at her ears blew now in the wind as she left the stable.

There was more on her mind than a blue-eyed devil of a man. There was Freddy again. Just what was he up to now? She had discovered that he had gone out early. A thorough inquiry at the stables gave her an uncomfortable sensation. Indeed, he had left her a message that he did not want his Maxie to worry for he would be back at the Grange by mid-afternoon. This, very naturally, and almost immediately worried Maxie. Where had he loped off to this time? Why was he keeping it a secret?

The trouble was that she knew Freddy, and knowing Freddy made her uneasy!

Maxie sighed and studied the sky. She would have preferred to ride. However, the clouds still lingered in masses of threatening darkness. Best then to stick to the original plan and allow their groom to drive them in the barouche. At least it wasn't the out-dated coach that her aunt always preferred them to use. Her aunt had left Huntly neatly wrapped within its enormous confines earlier that morning.

So engrossed in these scattered thoughts was she, that she never heard footsteps at her back as she started up the first steps to the front door of the house. All at once, wide hands were encompassing her trim waist. She was startled into turning with a short yelp, as Doctor John laughed and quickly released her.

"Forgive me. I wanted to surprise you, not startle you," he said softly.

Claire stopped at the large gothic framed mirror in the hall and adjusted her straw bonnet until she was satisfied. She regarded her tall, slim frame and decided her pale yellow ensemble was perfect. Well satisfied, she started for the door which Peltons had already moved to hold open for her. She pulled on her kid gloves as she stepped outside. There the sight of Doctor John and Maxie in what appeared to be close conversation brought her up short with a start. She stood a moment uneasy about breaking in on their tête-à-tête. She wasn't quite happy about the singular attentions Doctor John was directing toward her cousin. There was something she couldn't name, something that troubled her, something she had never really noticed before. Perhaps she was being absurd? Perhaps she was simply jealous because he had transferred his solicitude from herself to her cousin?

Maxie and Doctor John were talking about her progress on her latest collection of short stories. Maxie sighed. "It is very difficult these days. For one thing, I must always wait till bedtime so I will be alone and uninterrupted." She shook her head. "I am glad that Mr. Evans has given me all the time I need, for apparently it will take longer than my last work."

"If it were up to me," said Doctor John softly, "I would provide you with your very own room. A place where you could go to be yourself. A room made of glass and overflowing with all your favorite plants and flowers." His hazel eyes were lit with sudden passion.

"A room made of glass? Would it not be chilly in the winter?"

"No, no." She was being deliberately provoking. Did she take him for a fool? He tempered his response. The mood must be soft, and so he maintained a quiet tone. "One wall would house a huge fireplace and on either side of it, shelves and shelves of all your very favorite authors, every book you have ever wanted, there at your disposal." He was very proud of the plans he had made for her comfort. He wanted her to see the advantages of a union with him.

"Good-morning," Claire said shortly, hurrying up to them, smoothing her tight-fitting gloves over her fingers.

Doctor John was irritated by Claire's interruption. Why was she forever about? He would have to arrange a meeting with Maxine where they could be alone. He smiled at Claire and said, with an inclination of his head, "Ah, you two wish to be off and I am detaining you?"

"Indeed." Claire answered in clipped tones, "We are on our way to town."

"Shopping again?" The doctor was surprised. It wasn't like Max to be forever at the shops.

"Noo," returned Claire. "We are meeting friends at the Sweet Shop for luncheon."

Doctor John was not satisfied. He felt they were lunching with Waremont and Sir Leigh. Outrageous that Mrs. Huntly would allow such forward behavior. No, just like her, for she wanted to secure advantageous marriages for her daughter and niece! She was an unethical creature. These thoughts triggered a wild sense of ill-usage. He felt his blood rage with anger.

Well, he would just see for himself! Smiling as best as he could at Maxine, he said, "Perhaps we may continue our talk at another time . . . when you are not too busy for me?"

She caught his gloved hand. "Dearest Doctor John, I shall never be too busy for *you.*"

Somewhat mollified, he allowed her a sad smile. "No? Then I am relieved."

As soon as Claire and Maxine were settled in the chocolate brown baraouche with its pretty yellow wheels, Claire leveled a frown at Maxie and said gently, "Max, I am no doubt absurd, but, I don't like the notion of you and Doctor John."

Maxie laughed. "Rest easy. Doctor John is a very dear, dear friend, and any girl should count herself lucky to win him. However, I am not in love with him, and you know, I *am* a romantic in spite of the fact that I choose to travel in a coach instead of riding to town in the rain." She laughed sweetly. "A romantic must marry for love!"

Waremont had the medical report tucked in his inner pocket as he and Sir Leigh walked towards the quay and Toby's boat. However they had not reached their destination when Toby coming out of a chandler's shop nearly ran them down.

Waremont held the man's shoulders and said, "Toby! Just the man we wanted to see."

"Eh, wot news 'ave ye?" Toby eyed them keenly.

"Come along, we need some privacy for this."

"The Sweet Shop," put in Kinnaid anxiously. "We are due there."

"Right then, we'll talk at the Sweet Shop," agreed Waremont.

"Lord bless ye, I never 'ad much use fer sweets—"

"The coffee will do you good, and at any rate, we shall all think clearer if our minds aren't muddled with drink," Waremont returned amiably as he led the way back towards the center of town.

The Sweet Shop's owner, Mrs. Pringle, might have been surprised to see the likes of Captain Toby walking in with two fashionable members of the aristocracy. However she shrugged over this for there was never understanding the vagaries of the gentry. They took a table and ordered coffee.

Toby sipped the dark black brew, watching with a raised eye as Kinnaid added both sugar and cream. He pulled a face and commented, "Shouldn't go maudlin yer insides wit all that."

"I tell you what, old fellow," said Kinnaid, "I'll try it your way, if you try it mine."

Toby snorted. "Lord love ye, lad, there ain't no way but my way."

Waremont interrupted their discussion on the pros and cons of black coffee. "Toby, I think I may know *why* Annie was murdered!"

Freddy was at his wits end. Desperation had been driving him all morning. He knew he had to find Sarah Jane Stone. Here he was so very close and he could not remember which country road held her friends' thatched cottage. He couldn't very well ride up and down every lane. That would take days. What was wrong with him? It hadn't been all that long ago when he had driven her to Lydd.

He looked up at the sky. He was deuced glad the rain had stopped for he had nearly been soaked through in spite of his rain gear. Well, he was getting weary of the chase. He hadn't wanted to show himself in town. Didn't want anyone to know he was poking about looking for Sarah. That wouldn't do? However, he could go in for a bite to eat? Damn, yes for he was ravenously hungry. The Ryans! That was their name. It came to him in a flash. He would ask after the Ryans' cottage without identifying himself. No one would be the wiser . . .

Maxie entered the Sweet Shop and opened her eyes wide to see Toby in deep conversation with Kinnaid and Waremont. This was very odd. She knew that both Toby and Sir Leigh were interested in finding Annie Bagner's killer, but, she had not realized they were actually working together so closely.

Claire wrinkled her nose and whispered, "Isn't that your seaman friend? What is he doing with—?"

"Shh," Maxie cautioned for the gentlemen in question had already turned to look their way.

Both Waremont and Kinnaid jumped to their feet, though it was Kinnaid who went forward to escort the ladies to their table. Toby was already shuffling away, stopping in front of Maxie to grin. "Well, now, where is that resty lad of ours off to this morning?"

"Freddy?" Maxie asked and she was concerned enough to take hold of Toby's sleeve. "I don't know. Oh Toby, did you see him?"

"Aye, though he didn't see me. He was on the Main Pike Road toward Lydd. What business 'as 'ee there I'm after wondering."

"He didn't confide in me, which has had me concerned all morning," returned Maxie content that Claire was engrossed with her new beau and couldn't overhear them.

"Don't fret over it, lass. There ain't a whole lot of bobbery fer 'im to fetch up in Lydd." Toby patted her gloved hand which was still clutching at his worn dark wool coat.

"No, I don't suppose there is." She smiled tentatively as she released him and turned to find a pair of twinkling blue eyes scanning her face. Waremont took her elbow, nodding to Toby as he moved her away from the center of the shop. "May I take you to our table?"

"Oh, Sir Leigh, hallo." She was smiling up at him and all too aware that her knees felt weak. Faith, he was so handsome, so mesmerizingly . . . Stop! Stop it, you silly girl!

There were other people coming into the Sweet Shop so she readily agreed and took her leave of Toby who gave Waremont a conspiratorial glance and said, "Tomorrow then?"

Their look was not missed by Max. She rounded on Waremont and demanded, "Tell me. Something has happened! You have seen the medical report!"

"Quiet now, child." He saw her seated and pulled up a chair very close to her own.

"Tell me, what did it say?" Maxie asked impatiently. Her tone drew the attention of her cousin and Kinnaid who waited in sudden quiet. Waremont knew that she would not be put off. He looked about before saying on a whisper, "Apparently young Annie was compromised. She was carrying a child."

"What?" shrieked Maxie.

"Hush!" cautioned Waremont.

"Well, that is dreadful, "said Claire who did not at all approve.

"What is more dreadful, Miss Huntly, is that the man who managed to disgrace this child is undoubtedly the very man who must have killed her. Think further, if you will. If he killed her rather than find a way of helping her, he would do it again for he has even more at stake. That is why Sarah Jane Stone ran away. She knows who he is. By now, he must be aware of *her* as well . . ."

Chapter Twenty-Two

Maxie put down her pen and shoved her scribbling aside. She had been working furiously ever since they had returned from town. She hadn't wanted to think, she hadn't wanted to feel. For if she did, she thought she might go mad. It was *he!* Always, it was he. His blue eyes twinkling, laughing, glaring . . . and warm. His smile, endearing, engaging, genuine and directed at her.

She got up and went to her window. The sky had cleared and the sun was peeping out. Soon the afternoon would be gone and dusk would take over. What she needed was a walk. That was it. A nice brisk walk to clear her cobwebs. She would take a small basket of biscuits to Cyg.

She took up her dark blue cloak, fastened it round her shoulders, slipped her hands into her gloves and made her way down the backstairs to the kitchen. There she stole an armful of biscuits, deposited them into a basket while Cook wagged a finger at her, and hurriedly made her way outdoors.

It was a short walk, no more than six or seven minutes to the dock on the River Rother. Sadly, Cyg was nowhere in sight. Max plopped down onto the wooden planking, dangling her legs over the river. It was so beautiful here.

"Now, how did I know that I would find you here at this moment?" said a strong male voice.

Maxie looked round, aware all the while that she was trembling. What was wrong with her? A smile flickered over her troubled features. "Indeed, sir, how *did* you know?"

Waremont strode purposely toward Maxie and took her hands.

She did not refuse him. He pulled her to her feet and his voice was low, husky and full with his intent as he spoke. "Because, love, I sensed it. I felt it here." His hand moved to his heart and then he was holding her in his warm embrace. His blue eyes were looking into her dark violet eyes with feeling, and his kiss was a gentle touch of tenderness. Passion sure and intense was held in check as his lips parted against her own.

Even as Maxie melted to his touch, logic raised its ugly head and demanded answers. What are you doing? Maxie, wake up, girl! What are you doing? He will break your poor heart!

She pulled out of his hold and was surprised, perhaps almost disappointed to find that he immediately released her. It was so very vexing to find that it appeared so easy for him to let her go when every inch of her wanted to continue in his embrace. "Stop, please," she whispered.

"I can not honestly tell you I am sorry. I am not. I have wanted to do that now for sometime." He. said softly.

Maxie frowned and was attempting to put her thoughts in order and then into words when the sound of a horse snorting in the wind brought her head round. She was supremely irritated to find Doctor John barreling down on them. Why was he forever seeking her out?

"I should not be seen here alone with you." Waremont said as much to himself as to her.

"No, please don't go." She wondered what the deuce was wrong with her. Doctor John was her friend, and yet she knew she did not want to be left alone with him. Her instincts were at war with her logic. This was Doctor John. She should be ashamed of herself.

"What is it, Maxie?" Waremont eyed her.

Doctor John's smile was cold as he glanced toward Waremont and greeted him. "Good afternoon, my lord. No doubt you are here to see how Maxie's young swan is coming along."

Maxie giggled. "Hallo Doctor John. Cyg doesn't seem to be about, but you are mistaken. This is Sir Leigh Kinnaid."

The doctor seemed taken aback. "No. How can that be when we have just introduced ourselves the other day? Is that not so, Lord Waremont?"

Waremont felt the earth shake beneath his feet. Never before had he been so trapped. Never before had he cared so very much. He inclined his head, and turned to Maxie. "Allow me to explain."

Of course. This is what she had known all along. This

was the thing that had been nagging at her all along. Here was Lady Waremont's son. This was the man the lady had described to her in such detail. Well, he and his friend had played a neat little jest on a country family. Was he proud of himself? Her heart felt wrenched. "Explain? How could you *ever* explain?" She turned and started off, holding back the tears as she apologized to Doctor John.

"Please forgive me, I must return to the house . . ." She was almost running. She could hear Waremont's voice at her back, calling her name, but she didn't look back. How could she? Her world was suddenly falling apart. Everything had been nought but a joke.

Doctor John watched as Maxie ran off. He knew better than to follow. He heard the desperation in Waremont's voice as he called after her. His mind started clicking away. He had followed Maxie and Claire to town earlier that day, and discovered that their luncheon had been a coze with Lord Waremont and Sir Leigh in attendance. It had infuriated him. How dare both Claire and Maxie mislead him? How could he trust Maxie now? She, too, had her head turned by wealth and power. What to do? He had spent the remainder of the afternoon in a quandary of indecision. Just how would he handle Maxie with stars in her eyes? He had felt driven by pure vexation, but he had wanted to keep a clear head. He had ridden to the dock in the express hope of finding Maxie there alone. He had so wanted to talk to her.

Suddenly, matters seemed to be working themselves out. He wasn't sure just what had occurred. He didn't quite completely understand just what had taken place, but, it was obvious that Lord Waremont had erred in some way and had been found out. Indeed, it appeared that Rake Waremont would get no more of Maxie's time! Ha!

However, he had to be careful and proceed warily. He had to know just what all this was about. Cautiously and in a quiet tone he inquired, "What, my lord, is going on?"

"It is a matter between Miss Tarnover and me," Waremont answered curtly.

"Indeed? From what I could fathom you have been addressing Miss Tarnover and the Huntly family under another identity. To what end?"

"What *I* have been doing, Doctor Wiltshire, is my own affair." said Waremont. He nodded in dismissal and walked briskly away.

Doctor John watched him leave and smiled to himself. Very well, he would hear the tale from Maxie on the morrow. At any rate, he had no more to fear from the London roués! They had managed to ruin themselves in Maxie's eyes without any outside help.

Maxie gave her cloak to Peltons and ran into the house and up the stairs like a woman crazed. She went directly to Claire's room and pounded on the door. The resonant sound effectively snapped Claire out of her delicious daydream and brought her quickly to her door which she opened only a very little bit. Maxie pushed passed her then paced a moment while her cousin looked on in some concern. *"Maxine?* Whatever has you so angry?"

Max noticed the door was still wide open and though she now knew of Waremont's treachery, she was not yet ready to betray him to her aunt and uncle, "Claire, close the door!"

"What is wrong with you?"

"What is wrong? I shall tell you in a moment. Close the door."

Claire did as she was bid and then folded her arms akimbo to reprimand her cousin, "Really, Max, all these dramatics—"

"We have been duped. We are no more than green country girls and they have played a famous jest at our expense."

"Who? What? Max . . . *make sense.*"

"I can't make sense because there is no sense to it all." Max stopped a moment and frowned at Claire. This was going to hurt her cousin who had formed a definite attachment for the man she believed was Waremont. Still, she had to be told. "Claire, they switched identities. I don't know why, but that is what they did."

"Who? Who has traded identities?" Clearly Claire had not the smallest notion.

"Lord Waremont and Sir Leigh Kinnaid are not what they seem," said Maxine in scathing accents. "In fact, the man you believe to be courting you has been doing so under a false name." Saying it aloud pained her as much as she knew it was going to pain Claire to hear it.

Claire went white. "Why are you saying this? Why would you wish to hurt me so?"

Maxine went to hold her shoulders, but Claire shrugged her off saying, "I want you to leave my room. *Now!*"

"Claire, listen to me. They came from London and perhaps they thought they would return before they were found out. They switched names. Waremont became Kinnaid and Kinnaid became Waremont. They have played a May Game with us, for their own private entertainment." Maxie shook her head and was angry with herself for a tear had formed and started down her cheek. She didn't want to cry. Why should she cry? They were worthless beings, playing with other people's feelings for a jest.

"But ... why?"

"I don't know. We have often heard that the *haute ton* are forever doing outlandish things out of boredom. Claire, everything they have said to us, everything they have done has been a lie."

"No, Lord Waremont and I ... he would not ..." Claire clasped her hands together and then nearly pleaded, "But he loves me. Maxine, I know it ... feel it. He could not have been pretending."

"He is not Lord Waremont. He is Kinnaid. He has courted you under false pretenses. It has all been a lie ... a terrible lie, because the rest of the town, Doctor John included knows them by their true names." Maxie grabbed Claire's arms and shook her then as though to bring her to reality.

"Maxine . . . I think I want to die."

Maxine's arms went around her and she held her for a long moment, "No, my dear. You don't want to die. You want to tell them to go to—"

"Maxine!" Claire cut her off sharply and then burst into tears.

As Maxine tried to comfort her she thought of the man now known to her as Lord Waremont. His blue eyes twinkled and she shook her head against such wiles. Lies . . . everything had been lies! The only truth she had been left with was that she was undeniably, uncontrollably, madly in love with him!

Chapter Twenty-Three

Freddy scratched on Maxie's door and waited. He knew she was in her room. Why the deuce wouldn't she answer him? They were due downstairs soon for dinner and he needed to talk to her first. He knocked. "Max, please. I have to talk to you. Max, please don't be angry with me? I shall tell you everything now, I swear that I will. May I come in, Max?"

Maxie wiped her eyes and blew her nose into her handkerchief, "Yes, Freddy, do come on."

He heard the tone and said on a low note, "Oh-oh." But he opened her door and walked into the fire, hands up in the air. "Before you say anything . . . I just didn't want to wake you this morning when I left and I couldn't very well have left you a message for all the world to hear."

"No, but, you could have written me a note and slipped it under my door," Maxie said sweetly.

"Well, yes." He grinned sheepishly. "I didn't think of it."

She sighed. "Right then, Frederick. Just where have you been all day?"

"Maxie. All at once I remembered something important. I once gave Sarah Jane Stone a ride to some friends of hers in Lydd. Thought I might find her there so loped off after her this morning."

"Faith!" Maxie jumped to her feet, momentarily diverted. "Was she there?"

"Well, I couldn't find the right road, so I went into town and described the place to the smith, not mentioning Sarah Jane you see, and he gave me its direction. Neat little thatched cottage. Went there. They wouldn't let me in and they said they hadn't seen Sarah Jane in a long while."

Maxie slumped. "Oh."

"Max, they weren't telling me the truth. I know she is there."

"How do you know?" She frowned at him.

"Well, the last time they were the friendliest people, grateful to me for having driven her all that way. They invited me in, made me welcome, gave me tea and cake. This time they scarcely opened their door a crack and acted as though they didn't even remember me." He shook his head. "Max, they were scared."

"Of you?" Maxie scoffed.

"No. I don't think of me, but perhaps they were afraid I had been followed. Max, I know that she is there."

"Well then, she knows who Annie's killer must be. She knows and she is frightened for her own life. Why else would she hide like that?"

"It is exactly what I think, Max." He hesitated and then said, "She might show herself to you though."

"Why? I don't see that. I only knew Sarah Jane in passing. We never spoke beyond a greeting."

"Yes, but you are a girl. She might trust another female. And besides, you have a knack of getting people to do what they should, even when they don't wish to. You have to go to Lydd and ask Sarah to come forward. I have no doubt that you will convince her," he said grinning at her amiably.

"Have you told Toby?" she asked.

"No, I haven't seen him yet today. I came straight home because it was so late and I didn't want you worried." He eyed her shyly.

Maxie hugged him then and said affectionately, "Oh Freddy, thank you for that. As to all of this . . . we must think it out thoroughly. We don't want Sarah Jane bolting out of reach, do we?"

"Zounds no!"

"Precisely. It could be that if I go to Lydd now, just after you, they might feel threatened. There is no saying what she might do then," Maxie said quietly.

"By Jupiter! I never thought of that," ejaculated Freddy much struck. "Might she run off now? After I was there nosing about. Have I ruined everything?" He was much disturbed by this notion.

"I don't know. I just don't know, Freddy. Perhaps not. We'll just have to wait and see."

"Well, I don't think I gave it away that I didn't believe them. Said that I was disappointed that she wasn't about and took my leave." He puffed up with some pride. "Thought to fool them you see. May have served."

"That was very clever Freddy-lad. Come, we had better not keep your parents waiting."

"Yes, but Max, what are we going to do?"

"We are going to eat our dinner, play at whist, go to sleep and see what the morning holds. More than that, I can not tell, for in truth Freddy, I don't have any answers."

Sarah Jane Stone was in fact seriously considering bolting and rushing off via stage to London. Her friends had convinced her to stay. There were too many dangers out there in the open. They told her that at least at their cottage no one could actually harm her. What? Did this murderer think he could come and kill them all? She laughed uneasily at herself, and agreed that they were right.

Still, the sound of Freddy's voice inquiring so boldly after her sent a chill up her spine. Her poor Annie, her poor Annie murdered so callously, and by someone all the village knew and liked. How would she make anyone believe her? How?

The air was heavy. The sky was a dreary shade of grey and a hard driving wind was shaking leaves off the trees and bending the tall pines. The weather held no invitation for man or beast. However, Kinnaid and

Waremont donned their caped greatcoats and braved the elements.

They rode in silence for a few moments, each lost to his own deeply disturbing thoughts until Kinnaid asked, "Seth, what if they won't receive us?"

"Then we shall try again this afternoon and again tomorrow, and again and again," said Waremont resolutely. "Depend on it, Leigh, in the end, we will find a way."

"Do you think so? I am dreading this, Seth. I still don't know how I will explain. Can't we do this thing in the same room with both the girls present at the same time?"

"It may be that we shall have to. However, I prefer to take Maxine aside," said Waremont quietly. He had known yesterday when his mouth had finally closed on hers. He wanted Maxine Tarnover with all his being. He was not going to rest in this until she knew it, understood it, accepted it. He was sure she must feel the same. She had responded to his kiss, she wouldn't be able to deny that. Bah! Women were always looking for more. Women always had to muddle everything with love. She would want to know about love, about forever. How would he answer that? Never mind. That was another issue. First, she would want to know the truth!

Waremont was bound to be sadly disappointed for he would not find Maxine at home. She and Freddy were already on their horses and on their way to town to visit Toby. They were riding quietly, in part because Maxine was not her usual bubbling self. And though Maxine did not notice it, Freddy was notably silent. He had caught a chill during his ride to Lydd in the rain the previous morning and was feeling its ill effects.

By the time they had given their horses over at the livery and walked the short distance to Toby's boat, Freddy was coughing. This brought Maxie's head round. "Freddy, are you ill?"

"Nonsense. Just a tickle in my throat." He waved it off. "Look there is Toby." He pointed to a tavern where Toby often spent his time with his cronies. He put up his arm and waved vigorously which brought on a fit of racking coughs.

Maxie was now concerned. "Frederick Huntly, you are ill!"

"I am not," he said firmly.

Toby was upon them and nodded as he led them towards his boat. He said on a low note, "Well then, I'm glad ye be 'ere. Freddy, I been told yet one more thing mayhap ye should've told me yerself."

"What is that, Toby?" Freddy asked.

"Jest 'ow friendly was ye wit Sarah Jane Stone, tell me that lad?"

Freddy's eyes opened wide. "Now what? No one can say I ever kissed her for that is a bold-faced lie. *I never did!*"

"Why would anyone say you had been kissing Sarah Jane?" demanded Maxine in some surprise.

"No, that ain't what they say, but they do say they saw ye jesting and laughing wit 'er more often than not." Toby shook his head. "Kissing one, laughing wit the other and me, never knowing about either. There is some saying ye was more of a lady's man than anyone knew and they be looking ye askance."

"What are you talking about?" Maxie expostulated. "Freddy, what is going on?"

"Look, forget about it!" snapped Freddy irritably, "We came here with some important information. Max thought we should discuss it with you."

"What would that be?" Toby looked to Maxie.

"Freddy thinks he may have found Sarah Jane Stone." Max put it simply though she was still eyeing Freddy thoughtfully and wondering what Toby had meant.

"Lord bless ye, don't be saying it so loud, not if ye want the girl alive in the morning!" snapped Toby as he looked around. Then quietly he asked, "Did ye speak wit 'er?"

"Not exactly," said Freddy rubbing at his forehead. He opened his riding coat.

Maxie watched him and reached to touch his cheek but he pulled out of range.

"Not exactly? Whot then?" Toby was impatient.

"Freddy went to Lydd because he once gave Sarah Jane a ride there to stay with some friends of hers. They have a thatched cottage just outside the village. They refused to allow him in, and denied that Sarah Jane was with them." Maxie sighed. "Do you know the cottage Toby? Do you know these people?"

"Aye, know 'em. She did right if she went to the Ryans. They'll keep 'er safe enough." Toby was frowning. "Wouldn't show 'erself to ye, Freddy? Now, I'm wondering why."

"I can only guess that she is afraid of being found." Freddy offered as he pulled a face. "Max thinks Sarah might show herself to you. She says that Sarah probably believes I am too young to trust with her life." He shrugged. "If anyone wants to know what *I* think, Max is the person for this job. I may look too young to know about such things, but, in my humble opinion, girl to girl, Sarah might feel easier?"

Toby snorted out a short laugh. "Ye may just 'ave a point there, and Freddy-boy, seems ye know a mite more about the ladies than I thought."

At Huntly Grange Lord Waremont and Kinnaid were taken to the library to await Miss Huntly's answer to their request for an audience with her and her cousin.

Peltons reappeared at the library door and though he disliked any show of emotion, he allowed a hint of the discomfort he felt to display itself in the set of his thin lips as he advised the two waiting gentlemen that, his young mistress, Miss Claire Huntly wished them to know that Miss Tarnover was not at home to receive them and that while she, Miss Huntly, did not wish to answer for her dear cousin, Miss Huntly wanted them to know that *she* never wished to be subjected to their company ever again in her lifetime!

Kinnaid turned to Waremont. "Did you hear that? Did you hear that? Now, what are we to do?" He turned to Peltons. "You must return to Miss Huntly and tell her that my life is over. If she won't receive me and hear me out ... I shall die."

"Very good, my lord." Peltons thought he, too, would die. This was completely mortifying. How would he live through this ordeal? Did not these young, eccentric members of the aristocracy realize *he* was a *butler?*

"Peltons, we will go now, but you may tell both ladies that we shall return, and return, and return ... until they receive us, and at least allow us the opportunity to explain." Waremont stopped a moment. "One other very important thing; I shall rely on you to tell Miss Maxine Tarnover something for me? Please, Peltons, remind her that in the interest of fair play, every condemned man should be allowed by his judge to tell his side of the story."

"Very good, sir." said Peltons who was feeling rather condemned himself.

Chapter Twenty-Four

There was a low mist forming over the marsh and the mild wind only served to whip it into a thickening salty fog. Maxine felt the sea's chill touch her cheeks and raised a brow for the denseness of the fog seemed to closet them quickly with its rolls of smoky white mist. Early darkness began to descend upon them as mist floated up from the earth and seemed to drip from the sky. Maxie looked round with a smile, for the Romney Marsh mists were not uncommon. She watched the mist move in on them, engulfing them in its stillness. It had an eerie feeling and Max touched her face which felt cold and wet from the damp. She was therefore surprised when Freddy stopped his horse to say, "Max . . . hold up a minute . . . want this deuced coat off . . . so . . . hot."

Maxie eyed him worriedly. Freddy's cheeks were flushed and his eyes were not focused. He looked to her as though he had a fever. She attempted to discourage him from removing his coat, saying soothingly, "Freddy, please, don't take it off. Suffer it just a moment longer. We shall be home in a thrice, and then we shall get you into bed, depend upon it, for I can see that you are ill." She frowned at him. "Please don't be a silly and think you can talk fustian to me, for it won't fadge!"

He eyed her irritably. "Always telling me what to do. Not m'mother, you know."

"No, I, thankfully, am not." teased Maxine. "I am your friend."

He had a sunny disposition and rarely stayed vexed about anything more than a moment or two. He grinned at her. "Friends don't nag."

Maxie saw him slipping from his horse and immediately brought her horse along-side his gelding. She couldn't panic. She had to maintain her good sense. She nudged her horse closer still, and took his reins as she steadied him on his horse, saying loudly and authoritively to get his attention, "Freddy, put your head down on dear Whisper's neck! Do it! That's right. Good lad." What was she going to do?

Doctor John guided his cob through the grassy field at a slow pace. The fog was making it increasingly difficult to pick a path safe from dangerous pits and underground caverns made by the ever vigorous moles and their like. However, the sound of Maxine's voice had him on the alert and suddenly he had Max and Freddy in sight. It was clear that something, though, he could not tell just what, seemed to very wrong. He hurried his pace across the field to where they were stopped on the road and called, "What is it, Maxine?"

"Oh, Doctor John! Thank goodness you are here. Freddy is ill, with a fever, I think." Even as she spoke, Maxie was jumping off her horse. Freddy was slumped across his horse's neck. Doctor John helped her hold Freddy in his saddle. "This is all my fault. I should have noticed he wasn't himself." She was very near to tears. "Doctor John, he hasn't been right all morning. He has been coughing and . . . I should have known. I did know!"

"There, child. He will do. It is probably no more than a chill. Once we have him home and in his bed resting comfortably, he will come around and be himself by morning." Doctor John spoke softly to her, pleased to be in this position of command.

"Yes, yes, we must get him to bed."

Slowly, with Max leading the three horses and John supporting Freddy they returned to the grange.

Maxie ran up the steps and as Peltons opened the door, anxiously calling for help. This, very naturally set off a series of frenzied events. Almost immediately two footmen appeared to help carry Freddy within. This caused something of a commotion, which produced Mrs. Huntly. She came out of the drawing room demanding to know what all the noise was about and spied her son being carried unconscious up the hall stairs. In a panic, she called out his name, felt unwell and started to reel backwards. Unfortunately, in doing so, she banged her head on the extended arm of a hall antique statue that she had never really liked. She screeched in startled pain and proceeded to fall in a faint.

Peltons ran to his mistress who revived herself enough to shakily call for hartshorn. Faithfully he fetched it and began to administer it when the lady's maid appeared on the scene. She proceeded to snatch the hartshorn away from Peltons advising him icily that it was *her* job to attend to Mrs. Huntly. Peltons gladly though stiffly bowed himself off and thought that the morning was progressively becoming worse.

It was another thirty minutes before the house was once again running smoothly. Doctor John bled Freddy and suggested that he be sponged with lukewarm water to reduce his fever. He had hoped to get Maxine alone in conversation. There was so much he wanted to know, so much he needed to know. However, he could not find a moment in which he could easily manage such a feat. It was all too obvious that she was preoccupied with Fred's condition. Doctor John wanted her undivided attention; nothing less. Gently he touched her shoulder and then cupped her chin. "Now, Maxine, I know what it is in this household. I don't want you run ragged looking after him. There are servants enough that may do that. I shall return tomorrow morning and see how he goes on."

"Thank you so much, Doctor John," Maxine said sincerely as she reached up and placed a kiss on his cheek. "Whatever would we do without you?"

He smiled warmly at her and inclined his head. "It is my hope that *you* shall never try to find an answer to that."

* * *

As Max rushed up the stairs once more she encountered Claire who clutched Maxie's hand. "Thank goodness, you were with Frederick when he took ill. Maxie,
if he had fallen from his horse, out there in the fog, by
himself he might not have been found for hours. He
could have—it is unthinkable what could have happened!"

"Yes, yes . . . but never mind that now." said Maxine
impatiently, "I must see to him. Have you gone to your
mother? She was asking for you?"

"Indeed, she is resting now. This was such a shock to
her." Claire frowned. "Mother has such delicate sensi-
bilities. And with Papa away—

"Hmm, it is a lucky thing you are more like your father," said Maxine ever frank.

"Maxine!" objected Claire, and then quickly putting
this aside, added, "Oh, Max, with all the confusion, I
am certain that Peltons has not told you, but *they* were
here this morning, requesting to speak to us. In fact—"
she sighed almost longingly—"Sir Leigh, and it is so odd
to call him Sir Leigh, when I was so used to calling him
Lord Waremont, but never mind, Sir Leigh it is, sent a
message to me through Peltons saying he would *die*. Can
you imagine? He said he would die if I did not accept
to see him."

"And did he?" asked Maxine dryly.

"Oh, Maxine, there you go again. How I used to
think you a romantic figure, I can't imagine, for there
isn't an ounce of romance in you!" snapped the lady in-

censed. "Of course, he did not die. However, how sweet of him to wish to ... for *my sake*."

"You mean, how clever of him to say so," said Maxine on a cynical note. She was not about to be fooled again.

Claire frowned. "Yes, but, why bother to say anything?" She wagged a finger. "If he genuinely did not care, he could just go on his merry way and forget all about me." She paused a long moment before proceeding, "I have given this a great deal of thought. After all, there must have been a reason for them to play such a dastardly trick." She released a long sigh. "And what Mama and Papa will say when they discover it, I am afraid to think."

"What difference can it make? We shall never see them again," said Maxine stopping to turn on her cousin, her hands on her hips.

Claire looked away. "I ... suppose you are right ... but, Maxine ... I feel ... truly that if I never see him again, *I* shall die." A pent up sob escaped her throat and spluttered from her lips as she turned and ran in the direction of her room. Maxine looked after her and said loudly, "Indeed, Claire, I may have been mistaken and you are much more like your mother than I had guessed! Here is your brother ill in his bed and all you can think of is yourself. Has the world gone mad?" Even as the thought was uttered another came to haunt and it was of Waremont. Waremont? Had she always thought of him as Waremont? Something deep inside her had always questioned his identity. She had always known that he was not what he seemed. Heavens! Now she was doing it! She was putting her own petty problems before that of Fred's very real one. Indeed, but, her heart was certainly breaking. Hurriedly she crossed the long corridor to her young cousin's room where she found Mr. Huntly's valet hovering over Freddy's limp form. She smiled reassuringly at the elderly fellow as she whispered, "Have you prepared the mixture?"

As an answer, he brought the basin to the bed and said, "Just as you asked, with a cup of rose water, miss."

Maxie took a wad of linen and dipped it in the mixture before easing back Freddy's covers and starting its application, cooing to him softly all the while. Here was Freddy, helpless and feverish and still she was thinking of a devil with blue eyes!

Chapter Twenty-Five

Maxie sat up in her bed. Was it really morning? Ugh, what an awful night it had been. Claire had put aside her unhappiness and had appeared at Freddy's bedside to relieve her cousin but even so Max had not really been able to sleep. They had taken turns rubbing Freddy down in the hopes of breaking his fever. However, it had only served to give him a modest comfort. His tossing would subside for a time and then his fever would return. Owens had taken the last shift, three hours ago so that Max and Claire could get some sleep.

Max put a hand to her head for she was more than just tired. She was heartsick and confused, made more so by the intelligence she had received from Peltons during the evening. She had left Claire in charge of Freddy, for she had needed to stretch her legs and went to the kitchen in search of tea. She was met there by Peltons who jumped to his feet and advised her that they were all concerned for their dear Master Frederick. Maxie smiled to thank him and would then have moved on had he not detained her. "Excuse me, Miss Maxie?"

"What is it, Peltons?" Maxie managed for she felt almost too fatigued to listen.

"Lord Waremont was here this morning."

"Yes, Miss Claire mentioned it to me."

"Yes, but, he had a specific message he wished me to convey for him to *you.*"

"I don't wish to hear it." She looked away, then as Peltons was about to bow himself off she asked, "Very well, what was the message?"

"He wanted you to know that he would return, and return, and return until you received him. And . . . well, he wanted me to tell you that in the interest of fair play, every condemned man should be allowed by his judge to tell his side of the story."

Maxie's fatigue had vanished in an instant. Her violet eyes flashed.

"Return will he? Hear his side of the story? How dare he? How dare he, Peltons?"

"Indeed."

"So then, you think I am right and should not hear him out?"

"If you think so, miss. It isn't really for me to say, is it?"

"Yes, but, Peltons, why should I listen to him?" Maxie pursued desperately.

"Always a good notion to hear all the facts," said Peltons.

She regarded him dubiously. "He might just tell me another absurd lie."

"Very true, Miss Maxie. One can never be too careful."

"Still, you are very correct . . . one should always be in possession of the facts . . ."

Maxie had wrestled with her decision all through the night, and still had not a clue if she would indeed receive Waremont. However, there was no time to bother about such absurdities when Fred lay helplessly ill in his bed. If only her uncle would return. She would feel so much better if he were at home.

Waremont pushed his plate of uneaten food aside and got to his feet. What he needed to clear his head was a ride. Kinnaid had not come down yet, and at any rate he was heartily sick of his friend's moaning. He had spent an ugly night of nightmares, tossing and turning and hard thinking. It had left him with a feeling of extreme desperation and determination. He was going to ride over to Huntly later in the day, and if he had to he would drag Miss Maxine Tarnover out of her room, she would hear what he had to say! She cared. He knew, sensed, felt that she cared. Had she not responded to his kiss? Tarnover was going to hear him out! He had to think clearly. Life, until now had always run smoothly. He had been relatively happy, had he not? Damnation, indeed he had. Now, all that was drastically altered. He had discovered that he lived in the anticipation of seeing Max, of hearing her voice, watching her violet eyes laugh, reveling in her infectious giggle. His mind was filled with Maxine. She was just a little fluff of country and she held his heart as no other ever had, as no other ever could and here ... he had hurt her as he had no other. How had things come to this pass? His horse had been brought to him from the stable and he mounted it, took the reins and immediately trotted off down the drive. He knew exactly where he was going!

Maxine had spent most of the early morning with Freddy. She had already bathed him twice when Claire appeared and going to her cousin declared, "Oh, Max, you are looking fagged to death! Here, go on and lie down for an hour. Freddy looks as though he is resting comfortably and I shall sit with him."

Maxie accepted the offer, but as she walked to her room, she changed her mind. What she needed was some fresh air, not her bed. Taking up her hooded cloak and her kid gloves she went down the backstairs to the kitchen. Hurriedly she put some muffins in a napkin before she rushed out into the morning sunshine. Oh, the soft cool breeze felt good! Her head was near to exploding. Her mind had turned into a jumble of worries and conflicts. Why hadn't Freddy's fever abated? Why had Waremont so ill-used them? Would Claire go into a decline for this fellow, Kinnaid? Indeed, she had never seen Claire like this before. Was it possible Kinnaid truly loved Claire? And Waremont? Just what did he want? Why had he taken such advantage of her? Why had he kissed her with such feeling? Why had he and Kinnaid exchanged identities? Lady Waremont had said her son had reason for the excesses he had embarked upon in his life. She had said he was wild to a fault, but she had also said that he had a good honest heart at bottom. Oh, she had so liked Lady Waremont. Could a woman like her have demon for a son? Had he just played a game that had gone awry? What should she do?

Before long, Max was at the dock throwing pieces of muffin to Cyg. She spoke softly to the swan and her voice trembled with unshed, but very ready tears. "My, my, Cyg. You are really growing, aren't you?"

"Indeed, he is," said a strong familiar voice at her back.

Maxie spun round. Here was her blue-eyed devil, her love, her heart-breaker towering above her and all at once she felt she couldn't breathe. The sky began to spin right before her eyes and the earth shook her off balance. A small cry escaped her lips and she knew she was going to faint.

"Maxie . . . sweetheart," said Waremont reaching for her as she collapsed in his arms. He bent with her, holding her just above the ground and balanced on his strong thigh. He stroked her face. "Max, my little love, what has happened?"

Maxie came round with a flutter of her lashes and a feeling of foolishness. Such weakness was not like her. "Forgive me. I suppose I was more tired than I realized." She attempted to rise but he held her in place, resting in his arms.

"Maxie, what is it? Tell me love? You look as though you have not slept."

She managed a rueful smile and a bantering sound tickled her voice in spite of their estrangement. "Really?

Well, if you had been up all the night because a devil had done you wrong—"

"No, no." He blanched. "Maxie, so I have, but, I mean to make it right. I swear!"

"Do not flatter yourself! This is not about you!" she snapped. "Please, help me to my feet."

He did as she asked. "Maxie . . . if you would allow?"

"No, at least not now. Freddy is very ill. Claire and I have been up most of the night and his fever still has not broken. I took a few moments to . . . to get some air, but I must return." She turned.

He reached for her and took hold of her arm. "I am sorry to hear that Freddy is unwell. If there is anything, anything at all that you need?"

"I should *trust* you to care for my needs?" She raised a brow. "Trust a man who calls himself friend in another's name? Should I want your help now, have I your correct name, my lord?" She started off, her chin well up.

He had her arm and turned her to him as he moved in and dropped a kiss on her lips. *"Trust in that,* Maxie. The rest will follow. I shall be on hand . . . for *you.* Just get word to me and I will come."

She looked at him then for a long moment. Why was he doing this? How could he look so sincere? She couldn't answer him. Again she started off, but he held her still in his firm grip. She looked round first at his hand on her arm and then up to his somber countenance.

He released her at once as though he were a chastised boy and said softly, "I shan't bother you anymore today, however, if I don't hear from you, I shall return to Huntly Grange tomorrow, if only to see how Freddy goes on. And Maxie . . . I will not leave Rye until you have heard me out."

"Indeed, Lord Waremont? I think that I have decided to hear you out. After all, it is what I deserve, is it not? Don't they say, once a fool, always a fool?"

He watched her and called out to her, "Maxine Tarnover! You were not fooled . . . not for a moment!"

She turned and almost smiled at him. "Oh, but, my lord, I concede that I was. However, that old saying; I mean to prove it wrong. So be forewarned, I shan't be taken in again." Maxie hurried away then, for suddenly she knew that if she continued to look into those blue eyes instead of running from him, she just might run to him!

Maxine returned to the house to find a sealed missive waiting for her in the library. She picked it up curiously. It was from Father McRay. With some excitement she broke the seal and held the ivory notepaper up to the light.

"My Dear Miss Tarnover,

Thank you and your cousin for your thoughtful visit. I have given your request much soul searching.

By now, you have read the contents of the medical report and may have come to a conclusion, as I have. We need not put it to paper.

I may not tell you who the father of the baby is.
That was a confidence of the confessional. However, Sarah Jane Stone was Anne's dear friend. I
have excellent reason to believe that Sarah Jane is
hiding herself away in the village of Lydd. For her
sake, she must come forward. She is a good Catholic girl, and knows what the right thing to do is,
but she knows that she is in grave danger. However, by now, this man knows of her existence. She
will not be able to hide forever, and, he can wait.
We must not allow him to claim another victim.
    Your Servant in Christ,
    Sean McRay"

Maxie felt as though she could scarcely breathe.
Freddy had been right. Sarah Jane was in Lydd! The library door opened and Claire entered, followed by Doctor John. Claire went forward and exclaimed gratefully,
"Oh, Maxie, thank goodness. We were just starting to
worry."

Doctor John went immediately to take both Maxine's
hands in his own firm grasp. "Maxine." He said her
name like a caress. The letter fell from her grip. He bent
to pick it up.

Max moved him away, holding his hands tightly.
"Freddy?"

He shook his head. "He hasn't yet responded to the
medicine I have given him but, at least he is no worse.
Frederick is strong. He'll come out of this." His eyes
moved involuntarily toward the letter laying negligently
on the area rug.

"Yes, strong and asking for you," stuck in Claire with a rueful smile. "Owens is hovering over him now, but nothing will do for Freddy, except you. The boy thinks you are the sun and the moon all wrapped in one!"

Doctor John frowned at her. "He can't expect Maxine to wait on him like a slave. She needs time to herself as well or I shall have another patient in this house."

Claire ignored this and dove in immediately. "Which reminds me, Doctor John. Mother is still in bed and wishes you to attend to her." She shook her head fretfully. "What father will think when he returns to this sad household?"

"Ah, that bump on the head giving her trouble?" He returned patronizingly.

"Yes. It left a nasty gash that is still bleeding now and then," said Claire.

Doctor John inched closer to Maxine even as he spoke to Claire. "Right then, I'll just go have a look in at your mother before I leave." However, he was now at Maxine's side, once more ready to take her fingers to his lips.

Maxine had already managed to scoop up the letter but, even as she refolded it, Doctor John was bending over her hand, softly saying her name. Quietly he bowed himself off, saying that he would return to look in on Freddy on the following morning.

Maxine had scarcely been able to contain herself. As soon as the door closed at the doctor's back, she took Claire's hands. "Claire, You may recall that I mentioned that Freddy and I visited Anne's priest?" Without waiting for her cousin's reply she hurried on. "Well, he has confirmed that Sarah Jane Stone may know the identity of the killer!" She waved the folded letter for emphasis.

"Oh, Maxie, how frightening. What are you going to do?"

"I don't know. I must think, but, right now I mean to see to our boy, Freddy. Faith, Claire, we can not allow his fever to continue!"

Chapter Twenty-Six

Morning came and the sun's September rays found Maxine slumped in a rocking chair not far from Freddy's bed. At her feet Melody was laying in a frog-like position, her long nose flat on the carpet. Freddy regarded the two and grinned fondly.

"Eh, you two. Looks like a fine morning for a run?"

Maxie nearly jumped at the sound of his voice and Melody got up to nuzzle her nose in his hand. "Freddy?" Max said getting up and going to him to immediately to touch his cheeks, his forehead. His complexion was better, his eyes were clearer and for once he did not feel hot!

"Oh, Freddy, you miserable wretch! We have been so worried."

"Sorry." He grinned. "Lord, but I am famished. What? Have you been starving me? How long have you had me in my bed? Has it been gruel and tea? I need a chop. I need eggs . . . ham and bread, chocolate. Food, Max, if you love me, you'll bring me food." He then swept his covers off and started to rise. "Nay, Melody and I shall fetch it ourselves." So saying, he promptly slumped back onto his pillows and took a moment to catch his breath.

"There, you odious child, are you happy? Absurd creature." Max patted Melody who barked in some concern. "Do not enact the clown again, Master Huntly, or you shall feel the wrath of my very dangerous temper!"

"Yes, ma'am." he said meekly.

She surveyed him wryly. "Yes, hunger is it? Right then, we shall have cook send up some porridge"—she put up a hand to forestall his objection—"with an egg to follow if you feel up to it."

"I suppose it shall have to do."

Maxie rang the bell and after this had been attended to, began reciting the names of the various visitors Freddy had during the last day, saying, "It is astounding how fast word got out about your ill-health. Toby heard. He came by yesterday afternoon and was determined to stay. I rather think he bunked down in the stables to wait on your recovery." She sighed. "He really is a sweet man in so many ways."

"Good old Toby." beamed Freddy well-pleased.

Then in some excitement she touched his shoulder. "Oh, Freddy! We got a letter from *Father McRay!*"

"Upon my soul!" ejaculated her cousin. "What does he say?"

She pulled out the letter from the pocket of her skirt and read him its contents. When she had done, he breathed "Whew! So, I was right. She is in Lydd!"

"Indeed. And I have quite made up my mind to it. I

shall ride there today and find her. We must put an end to all of this!"

"Not without me!" Freddy sat up straighter and winced.

"What nonsense is this? You can't leave your bed let alone the house." She touched him gently. "I shall do and I will come straight home to you and recount the whole."

"Yes, but—"

"Ah, here is your porridge."

All discussion was at an end because, along with the porridge came Freddy's father. He appeared at the doorway with a wide smile for his only son. "Frederick. I arrived this morning to the news of your illness." He held his son's shoulder. "I am glad to see that you are feeling more the thing." He looked across at Max. "Claire tells me you worked tirelessly. Thank you, my dear."

Maxie blushed and started for the door. "I did no more than either Claire or Owens. Well, Freddy, I leave you in good hands, I know. Now, I mean to bathe and change . . . and take a ride to Lydd. I shall see you as soon as I return."

Outside Freddy's door, Claire came up to Maxie to take her hands.

"Maxine, it isn't as dreadful as we thought! I have been with Papa, and he knows all. I think . . . I think that Sir Leigh loves me."

"What *are* you talking about?"

"Maxie, they confessed to Papa days ago. You see, Waremont is rather sought after by match-making mothers. He thought that his mother had sent him here because of *me*. They switched identities to spoil the sport . . . for a lark. They didn't think of the consequences. If Papa understands and forgives them, then I think we may as well. And Max, Papa means to handle Mama. Can you imagine?" Claire sighed happily, "He means to allow Sir Leigh to court me if I should wish . . . and I do. I do."

Maxie's brows were up. She had to think. So, Waremont and Kinnaid had actually gone to her uncle days ago. She would have to consider this aspect. However, she smiled at Claire and said softly, "If you are content to leave it at that, fine, though in truth, I still don't quite see."

"But you must agree that it makes a difference that they did go and confess the whole to Papa."

"Yes, I suppose." She shook her head. "At any rate, I haven't the time now. I want to bathe and change. There is something I must do and I should like to return here by this afternoon." She was thinking of Waremont. She wanted to receive him in the afternoon. She wanted to hear him out. She wanted— Never mind. First things first!

Maxie had taken a quick hot bath, donned her blue riding habit, tucked her long wayward dusky curls into a fetching display of disorder beneath a matching hat and was off to the stables. She was in a hurry and fidgeted as her groom prepared her mare for her. She wanted to leave before Doctor John arrived. She knew he would detain her. He might offer to accompany her to Lydd. A frown swept her forehead for she was touched with a twinge of guilt. Why did she feel this way about Doctor John? He was her friend. He had cared for Freddy. Yes, but, in his concern he was far too controlling—ah, here was her mare! She mounted outside the stable and with a wave to her groom urged her horse toward the path that ran through the woods.

Doctor John arrived at the Grange a few minutes later. He stopped by the stables and jumped nimbly off his gelding, handing the reins to the waiting groom. "How does young Huntly go on?"

" 'Ow ye'll be that 'appy ye will, sir. Fever broke. They say 'ee be on the mend."

"Excellent. I suppose, Miss Maxine is keeping him company."

"Miss just rode off," the groom replied easily.

"I see, no doubt she needed a morning ride after being couped up inside for so long." This did not greatly distress him. He was sure that Maxine would return before his call at Huntly was over. This had gone on long enough. He wanted her to understand that he meant her to be his wife. As soon as possible he would speak to her uncle.

Toby peeked in at Freddy's door and saw the lad resting against his pillows. "Sleeping are ye?"

Freddy looked round excitedly. "Toby! Famous! Come in here you old sea dog."

" 'Ere now. Is that any way fer ye to be speaking to yer elders and betters, halfling?"

"Toby, I am so glad you've come," said Freddy relaxing once more.

"Are ye now? 'Ow is that when ye've got a 'ouse full of good people looking after ye." He made a clucking sound of admiration. "On the top of that list I put Miss Max. Now that be a prime mort if ever there was one." He considered this for a second and added, "That sweet cook ye've got in yer kitchens, well now . . . she ain't 'alf bad either!"

Freddy laughed. "Now when did you develop an eye for the ladies?"

"As to that, never ye mind. Comes a time in every cove's life where 'ee thinks of 'aving a cozy 'ome." He sighed as he took up a hard back chair and planted himself.

"By Jove, Toby, wait till you hear!" ejaculated Freddy as he recalled his news. "The priest, Father McRay sent us a letter. He says Sarah Jane is in Lydd just as I guessed! What do you think of that?"

"Well now? Whot else did 'ee 'ave to say?"

"Toby, he knows who the father of poor Annie's baby is. Says that Sarah Jane knows as well."

"Well then, mayhap that is where I should be shaking m'shambles off to as soon as I leave 'ere later? Ye said she be staying with the Ryans?"

"Yes. Maxie is on her way there now, even as we speak."

"Never say so lad!" Toby snapped sharply. "I thought she 'ad more sense than that!"

"I wanted to go with her," said Freddy in some concern. "Do you think Max is in danger?"

"No. But she could be. I don't loike this. No, I don't."

Doctor John stepped away from Freddy's door. He had heard enough. There was no sense intruding on Freddy now when he seemed well and pleased to have a visitor. It was that seaman, Captain Toby! He could not approve of the fellow and when Maxine was his wife he surely would cut the connection.

He made his way down the main staircase. Really, all this talk of priests and intrigue? Just what had Freddy and Maxine to do with such matters? Just what had Maxine to do with a creature like Sarah Jane Stone? He knew the girl and she was nothing . . . nothing!

Well, he knew what his duty was. Maxine should not be riding unescorted all the way to Lydd! It was an outrageous thing to do just to visit with some lowly creature! He wouldn't have it. His wife was not to associate with such people. What was Sarah Jane? Nothing but the daughter of a Rye shopkeeper. He would ride after Maxine and return her safely home.

Waremont had waited for Maxine to send him word. The morning had progressed and he was unable to wait any longer. Sir Leigh was driving him mad. Thus it was they both took their horses and rode the short distance to Huntly Grange. As they approached the drive, Waremont noticed Doctor John riding away.

At the front door, Peltons said, "I gave your message to Miss Maxine, my lord." He then stiffened once more as he advised them that Mr. Huntly would receive them in the library.

"Indeed, I think you were a great help to my cause, Peltons," said Waremont graciously.

Peltons stoic countenance did not display his pleasure but his eyes twinkled all the same. He opened the library door wide and said their names with great resonance.

They were met there by Mr. Huntly whom they expected. However, they had not expected Claire to be present. Sir Leigh went forward almost spontaneously. "Claire?" He said in joyous accents.

"Sir Leigh," returned Claire softly as she went to place her hands in his.

Her father beamed happily at Waremont. "There, that is settled. You lads made a sad muddle of it while I was away you know."

"Yes, I know," said Waremont ruefully. He smiled. "The servants grapevine works faster than the post. The word is that Freddy is doing well."

"Indeed, why don't you go up and see for yourself?" Mr. Huntly offered jovially.

Waremont eyed his friend and Claire who were busily occupied with one another and grinned. "Good notion, that." As he made his way up the stairs he wondered where Maxie could be and hoped that he would find her in Freddy's room. Instead, he found Freddy and Toby looking worried.

"I hear you are—"

"Never mind that, m'lord," cut in Toby. " 'Ave a notion, we 'aven't time to waste."

Hurriedly, Freddy recounted the contents of the priest's letter and ended by saying that Max was on her way to Lydd. This distressed Waremont even more than it had Toby. He thundered, "What? Of all hare-brained notions." He then leveled a glance at Freddy. "Who else knows of this?"

"No one." said Freddy.

"You didn't mention it to the doctor when he examined you?"

"He hasn't been here yet this morning—"

"Yes, he has. I saw him turning out of your front drive. And when Kinnaid and I left our horses with your groom, he told us the doctor had already been and left."

Toby and Waremont exchanged glances and then looked at the half opened door. Waremont said on a low hard note, "When I approached your room Freddy, I heard you and Toby here without any difficulty because your door was open. Has it been open during all of Toby's visit?"

"Aye, it has," answered Toby promptly.

"Then Doctor John overheard us talking. He knows that Max is on her way to Sarah Jane in Lydd. My lord, I even told Toby she's staying with the Ryans."

"Never loiked the covey. Can't say why," stuck in Toby thoughtfully.

"The question then is, having come here why did he not stay?" Waremont shook his head as he moved toward the door. "Freddy, Lydd you say? I think I'll just head that way and make certain your cousin does not encounter any ... unpleasantness."

"Well, then there be nothing fer it, I'll be coming along wit ye. As it 'appens I know jest 'ow to get to the Ryans' cottage," said Toby firmly.

Freddy sat up and folded his arms in disgust. "Well, look at this! There is bound to be something havey-cavey going on, probably the best adventure of the year and I shall miss it!"

Chapter Twenty-Seven

Maxie had a great deal of trouble with Freddy's directions. She found herself in the village of Lydd before she was able to find someone to direct her to the Ryans' thatched cottage. Once there, she slipped out of her saddle and tethered her horse, noting that someone watched her from a window. She realized that she was suddenly nervous. She bolstered herself and resolutely knocked on the clean white door. A moment later a middle-aged woman with a white apron covering her dark gown appeared. She opened the door only a crack and said quietly, but politely, "Yes, what can I be doing fer ye?"

"You don't know me, but I am Miss Tarnover, from Huntly Grange. Father McRay advised me that he rather thought I would find Sarah Jane Stone staying with you."

"Bless him, but Father McRay is mistaken. She isn't here," said the woman as she moved to close the door.

Maxie was too fast for her. She had anticipated this

reaction and had hurriedly put out her hand, holding the door at bay. "Please, don't you see? It is imperative that I speak with Sarah Jane. This place is no longer safe for her. Can she keep running and hiding? Will she always live like that? She will have to, because if Anne's murderer isn't brought to justice, he will go after Sarah Jane!"

"Never mind, Miriam ... she be in the right of it." said Sarah Jane coming forward. She picked up her shawl and wrapped it around her thin shoulders as she stepped to the door. "Here now, miss, we best be stepping outdoors. The Ryans don't know nuthin' and fer their sake, I'd like to keep it that way."

"Yes, of course," said Maxine falling in step beside the tall thin girl. They walked for a few moments in silence, moving toward the back of the house where a small garden was flanked on three sides by fields. Sarah Jane tied her dark wool shawl in place and inched toward the fields as she looked around anxiously.

Maxie eyed the girl before saying, "I must tell you outright that I know Annie was with child."

"Aye, so she was. Oh Annie! How I miss her. We were friends forever. She wasn't a bad girl, miss, don't be thinking that," said Sarah Jane staunchly. "She fell in love, madly, and she thought he was going to marry her. She wasn't a fool, my Annie. She never let a man near her before. Not even your cousin. She slapped him roundly when he tried to kiss her. But this one, he was different, older. He knew what he was doing. When she told him they was going to have a babe, he only laughed at her." Sarah Jane shook her head. "It is all m'fault you know. I told her to go and tell him that if he meant to ruin her name, she would ruin his. My fault! Now my Annie is dead."

"Who did this to her?" Maxie was confused for a moment thinking of Freddy trying to kiss Anne.

"You won't believe me. No one will. He covered his tracks you see. No one ever saw him with Annie. He made sure of that. No one can prove he was the father ... not even me. I never saw him with Annie. I only know what she told me. That won't stand in court. What am I? A shopkeeper's daughter. What is he? A respected doctor."

Maxine stopped for she was frozen in place. She couldn't speak. She couldn't think. "What are you saying? A doctor? How could a doctor do such a thing?"

A shot from a horse pistol rang through the air shattering all coherent thought. It missed the women, but it served to halt all conversation. Maxine screamed and pushed Sarah Jane down to the ground, shielding her with her own body and whispering, "He wants you, not me." She looked round. They had walked too far from the cottage. He was in the thicket flanking their left. "Sarah, we shall have to move quickly." She held Sarah's hand and though she was trembling uncontrollably she was determined. "Stay low and run ... *now!*" As they moved, she covered Sarah's back, so when the next shot rang out, she felt it burn as it tore through the fine velvet of her riding jacket and singed her shoulder. Sarah screamed. "You are hurt, miss."

"It is nothing. Nothing. Come, we must work our way back to the cottage." The truth was that though it was

a nasty flesh wound, Maxie didn't feel it. All she knew
was that she couldn't allow this girl to be killed because
of her!

Waremont had the thatched cottage in sight. Toby's
horse, borrowed from the Huntlys, had been too slow to
keep up, so he had moved ahead, leaving Toby to bring
up the rear. He was motivated by pure instinct. He
smelled danger and his heart was on alert because his
beloved, his Maxine was right in that danger's path!
Love, right then, he admitted it to himself and now all he
wanted to do was take Maxie in his arms and admit it
to her! He was nearly crazed. Then he heard the gun-
shot and froze. He had to calm himself, study the elements. He did this and decided the shot had originated
from a thicket on the east side of the garden. He
jumped off his horse and carefully began stalking, his
own pistol cocked.

Doctor John was no longer thinking. He was acting
on unbalanced emotion. His enemies had to be elimi-
nated. The fact that Maxine would be a witness did not
matter to him. He would marry her. A wife could not
bear witness against her husband. She would forgive
him. He was only doing it for them, so they could be together. He had helped Annie, hadn't he? After all, she
would have brought misery on herself as an unwed
mother. He couldn't allow that, and he couldn't marry
her. How could he marry her? He was the son of a bar-

onet. The immediate thought that followed was that he had been the *bastard* son of a baronet. His father had acknowledged him. Oh, he had taken care of him, paid for his education, his clothes, his practice. He had been his father's only son and yet he had never been given his father's name! It didn't matter. He and Maxine would start their own family, the Wiltshires, their own family! He had to kill Sarah Jane now! He aimed, but Maxine got in the way. Suddenly he saw that he had missed Sarah Jane. His shot had found Maxine and he screamed in his fury, *"No!"* All at once he ran out of the thicket toward his enemy. Damn Sarah Jane. If his Maxine was hurt, it was all her fault. He would make her suffer before he killed her. She deserved it. She had been the one filling little Annie's head with absurdities about marriage! He would have already killed Sarah Jane if she hadn't been such a coward and run away when she heard of Annie's murder.

He was at their backs! Maxie's heart couldn't beat any faster and her mind suddenly went blank. What could she do? A familiar voice touched with the edge of madness broke through the air. "Stand, Sarah Jane. Here, Maxine, to me. *Now!"*

The girls turned and found Doctor John leveling a large horse pistol at them. He was still some distance from them. Maxie caught her breath. She couldn't believe it. Even when Sarah had said the man was a respected doctor, she couldn't believe it. No, no, not Doctor John? Her hand reached out toward him,

"Thank goodness you are here, Doctor John," she said, trying to buy time.

"Come here, to me, Max ... there is a killer loose, but *you* are safe with me."

"Yes, I know I am. However, I am hurt, Doctor John. Now that you are here, we can go back to the cottage and you can tend to this."

Sarah whispered at her back, "But, miss ... 'tis him I tell ye!"

He heard her and growled. "Don't listen to her filth! Annie was no better ... no better. She wanted to ruin me. Wanted to tell everyone what we had done. I couldn't allow that, could I, Max?"

Maxie felt sick, but she knew she had to humor him. "No, you couldn't, Doctor John. I know." She pushed Sarah Jane behind her. "We'll go home now, together." She was walking toward him slowly.

Doctor John was frowning. He was momentarily confused by conflicting sanity and madness. He knew he had to kill Sarah Jane. He also knew that he could not do so with Maxie's violet eyes looking directly at him.

"Stand aside Max," he said gravely as the madness won out.

Waremont's voice came strong, hard, and uncompromising. "Put the gun down, Doctor Wiltshire, and turn to me, hands high in the air."

Doctor John knew himself lost. It was over. Everything was over. As he turned he brought his gun round, firing without purpose. Waremont's reaction was instinctive as soon as he saw the doctor turn with his gun poised. Waremont fired and his shot did not miss its target. Indeed, it was over!

Maxie screamed as she ran to Waremont and threw herself into his arms. "You are here. You have come," she said with a sob.

"Did you doubt it?" He kissed her forehead, thankful she was safely in his arms, and then he saw her wound. "Maxine, oh my love, you are hurt." He was stroking her hair for her hat had fallen long before.

Toby appeared at that moment and looked at Doctor John's inanimate body. He moved to put a comforting arm around Sarah who had run to him as soon as he had arrived on the scene. He shook his head. "Well now, never loiked that covey!"

Epilogue

Maxie threw the last piece of bread she had with her to the young swan and said, "Well, Cyg, that is all for today." She turned and smiled to see Lord Waremont dismounting from his horse, dropping the reins in the tall grass and coming toward her. There was such a look in his blue eyes. It was so difficult to think that only yesterday she had watched a friend turn into a killer and a London rake turn into a hero! Her dark eyes twinkled as he reached for and received her hands.

"So you are here. I was up at the house first looking for you. When I didn't find you there, somehow I knew where you would be. How is your shoulder?" He bent and audaciously dropped a kiss there-on. "I am glad you are here."

She blushed rosily. "Better thank you ... and why?"

"Poor love, and coy monkey! You know very well all I want is to get you alone. My mother knew just what she was doing when she sent me to Huntly Grange. I am beginning to think you two had a plan hatched between you!"

"Whatever can you mean?" This time Maxie was surprised.

"It wasn't for Claire. She knew that was a match that would never take. It was for you. Maxie don't you see. My mother must have known after one hour in your company that I would meet my match in you. That was why she was so desperate to get me to visit the Huntlys."

"And was she right, my dear lord?" She grinned at him impishly. "Have you met your match?"

His blue eyes were alive with dancing lights. He took her into his arms and said huskily, "You know that I did. I love you, Maxie."

"Wait! There is so much you don't know about me. I just recalled, my lord, I am a published writer, though I have not used my own name. And it was Doctor John who helped me to keep my secret, and—"

"Maxie! Never say so?" He dropped a kiss on her lips and laughed. "Sweetheart, I am so proud."

"You don't mind?" she asked dubiously.

"Indeed, in the future, you shall use my name when you publish your works, my lovely future Lady Waremont!"

She threw her arms round his waist and put her head on his chest. "Oh, you are wonderful!"

"Yes, so I am, but, do you love me?" he asked on a grave note as his hand took up her chin.

"I love you . . ."

"What is my name, Max? Say my name." he asked her softly.

"I love you, Seth. That is your name, is it not?" Her violet eyes glittered.

He laughed and tweeked her nose. "Shall we have a winter wedding?"

"Brrhhh! Too cold. Better in the spring."

"Too far away. I have a need to have you with me always from now on. We'll have an autumn wedding. October is a wonderful time of year for a wedding."

"Do you think?" she asked slipping her hands up his chest to touch his face.

He crushed her to him and bent to kiss her mouth.

"Yes, I do think my little love."

ELEGANT LOVE STILL FLOURISHES –
Wrap yourself in a Zebra Regency Romance.

A MATCHMAKER'S MATCH   (3783, $3.50/$4.50)
by Nina Porter

To save herself from a loveless marriage, Lady Psyche Veringham pretends to be a bluestocking. Resigned to spinsterhood at twenty-three, Psyche sets her keen mind to snaring a husband for her young charge, Amanda. She sets her cap for long-time bachelor, Justin St. James. This man of the world has had his fill of frothy-headed debutantes and turns the tables on Psyche. Can a bluestocking and a man about town find true love?

FIRES IN THE SNOW   (3809, $3.99/$4.99)
by Janis Laden

Because of an unhappy occurrence, Diana Ruskin knew that a secure marriage was not in her future. She was content to assist her physician father and follow in his footsteps . . . until now. After meeting Adam, Duke of Marchmaine, Diana's precise world is shattered. She would simply have to avoid the temptation of his gentle touch and stunning physique – and by doing so break her own heart!

FIRST SEASON   (3810, $3.50/$4.50)
by Anne Baldwin

When country heiress Laetitia Biddle arrives in London for the Season, she harbors dreams of triumph and applause. Instead, she becomes the laughingstock of drawing rooms and ballrooms, alike. This headstrong miss blames the rakish Lord Wakeford for her miserable debut, and she vows to rise above her many faux pas. Vowing to become an Original, Letty proves that she's more than a match for this eligible, seasoned Lord.

AN UNCOMMON INTRIGUE   (3701, $3.99/$4.99)
by Georgina Devon

Miss Mary Elizabeth Sinclair was rather startled when the British Home Office employed her as a spy. Posing as "Tasha," an exotic fortune-teller, she expected to encounter unforeseen dangers. However, nothing could have prepared her for Lord Eric Stewart, her dashing and infuriating partner. Giving her heart to this haughty rogue would be the most reckless hazard of all.

A MADDENING MINX   (3702, $3.50/$4.50)
by Mary Kingsley

After a curricle accident, Miss Sarah Chadwick is literally thrust into the arms of Philip Thornton. While other women shy away from Thornton's eyepatch and aloof exterior, Sarah finds herself drawn to discover why this man is physically and emotionally scarred.

Available wherever paperbacks are sold, or order direct from the Publisher. Send cover price plus 50¢ per copy for mailing and handling to Penguin USA, P.O. Box 999, c/o Dept. 17109, Bergenfield, NJ 07621. Residents of New York and Tennessee must include sales tax. DO NOT SEND CASH.

WHAT'S LOVE GOT TO DO WITH IT?

Everything . . . Just ask Kathleen Drymon . . . and Zebra Books

CASTAWAY ANGEL	*(3569-1, $4.50/$5.50)*
GENTLE SAVAGE	*(3888-7, $4.50/$5.50)*
MIDNIGHT BRIDE	*(3265-X, $4.50/$5.50)*
VELVET SAVAGE	*(3886-0, $4.50/$5.50)*
TEXAS BLOSSOM	*(3887-9, $4.50/$5.50)*
WARRIOR OF THE SUN	*(3924-7, $4.99/$5.99)*

TODAY'S HOTTEST READS
ARE TOMORROW'S SUPERSTARS

Taylor—made Romance From Zebra Books

WHISPERED KISSES (3830, $4.99/5.99)

Beautiful Texas heiress Laura Leigh Webster never imagined that her biggest worry on her African safari would be the handsome Jace Elliot, her tour guide. Laura's guardian, Lord Chadwick Hamilton, warns her of Jace's dangerous past; she simply cannot resist the lure of his strong arms and the passion of his *Whispered Kisses.*

KISS OF THE NIGHT WIND (3831, $4.99/$5.99)

Carrie Sue Strover thought she was leaving trouble behind her when she deserted her brother's outlaw gang to live her life as schoolmarm Carolyn Starns. On her journey, her stagecoach was attacked and she was rescued by handsome T.J. Rogue. T.J. plots to have Carrie lead him to her brother's cohorts who murdered his family. T.J., however, soon succumbs to the beautiful runaway's charms and loving caresses.

FORTUNE'S FLAMES (3825, $4.99/$5.99)

Impatient to begin her journey back home to New Orleans, beautiful Maren James was furious when Captain Hawk delayed the voyage by searching for stowaways. Impatience gave way to uncontrollable desire once the handsome captain searched *her* cabin. He was looking for illegal passengers; what he found was wild passion with a woman he knew was unlike all those he had known before!

PASSIONS WILD AND FREE (3828, $4.99/$5.99)

After seeing her family and home destroyed by the cruel and hateful Epson gang, Randee Hollis swore revenge. She knew she found the perfect man to help her—gunslinger Marsh Logan. Not only strong and brave, Marsh had the ebony hair and light blue eyes to make Randee forget her hate and seek the love and passion that only he could give her.

Available wherever paperbacks are sold, or order direct from the Publisher. Send cover price plus 50¢ per copy for mailing and handling to Penguin USA, P.O. Box 999, c/o Dept. 17109, Bergenfield, NJ 07621. Residents of New York and Tennessee must include sales tax. DO NOT SEND CASH.